DON'T TELL

Other titles by Sandra Glover

DON'T TELL

SANDRA GLOVER

Andersen Press • London

For Sara, Rob, Ben and Sam.

First published in 2006 by
Andersen Press Limited,
20 Vauxhall Bridge Road, London SW1V 2SA
www.andersenpress.co.uk
www.sandraglover.co.uk

The right of Sandra Glover to be identified as the author of this work has been asserted by her in accordance with the Copyright, Designs and Patents Act, 1988

British Library Cataloguing in Publication Data available

ISBN-10: 1 84270 555 5
ISBN-13: 978 1 84270 555 1

Typeset by FiSH Books, Enfield, Middx.
Printed and bound in Great Britain by
Bookmarque Ltd., Croydon, Surrey

Chapter 1

Kirsty checked the time on her mobile. 20.03. Two minutes later than the last time she'd looked. She had to face it, Jamie wasn't going to show. No point phoning again but she did, only to find his mobile still turned off and the answering machine on at home.

Should she go in and watch the film on her own? No, it had already started and she didn't really want to see it anyway. It was some stupid, macho, action movie. Jamie's choice. There were other studios, of course, but it wasn't much fun watching a film on your own. She might as well catch the quarter past eight bus. Go home. Finish the work on *Romeo and Juliet* that was due in at the start of term. Throw herself into fictional love, in the absence of the real thing.

'You waiting for Jamie?'

She turned to see his mates, Ranjit and Tony, grinning at her. Surely he hadn't sent his mates to tell her she was dumped! Not even Jamie would do that. Would he?

'Er, no,' she said. 'I'd arranged to meet Sonja but she's just phoned to say she can't make it.'

'That's all right then,' said Tony, winking at Ranjit.

'What do you mean?' said Kirsty, wishing immediately that she hadn't asked.

1

'Nothin',' said Tony. 'It's just that we were with him in the park earlier and he said he had to go. Said he was meeting someone. We thought it might be you but then Laura turned up. You know, Laura Trent? Jamie's ex.'

Kirsty knew exactly who Laura was, so the lads didn't need to go into all the details but they were enjoying themselves too much to stop. Giving a graphic description of what Laura said and what she was wearing, or rather wasn't wearing, whilst Kirsty did her best to look uninterested.

'I think Laura still likes him,' Ranjit was saying. 'But Jamie won't do anything, will he? Not now he's going out with you.'

'No,' said Tony. 'He didn't look interested, did he, Ranj? Not really. He was trying to get away from her, I reckon. Yeah, I'm sure he was.'

Fortunately the boys had the sense to move before Kirsty was tempted to slap the smirks off their faces. She was about to cross the road, when she saw her bus pulling away from the stop. Oh great! The next one would be ages. Never mind, she'd walk home. Burn up some of her fury with a bit of exercise. It would only take forty minutes or so, less if she took a short cut through the park.

'Never walk home on your own,' her mother always said. 'And don't go through that park at night. It's not safe. You get all sorts hanging about in there.'

OK, so Mum was a born worrier, seeing dangers everywhere but with the recent muggings, maybe she

2

had a point about the park. Bags and mobiles had been snatched over the summer and, according to the local paper, one poor bloke had even been stabbed in the arm when he'd challenged his attacker.

Kirsty clutched her bag close to her side as she set off. There wouldn't be a problem. Not if she was careful. Stayed alert. Stuck to the roads. Avoided the park. There were plenty of pedestrians around at first but, as she left the town centre, she saw hardly anyone. Quite a lot of cars, admittedly, but very few people on foot. Was it true what her mum said? That most people were scared to go out at night?

It was already quite dark, with rain clouds hovering. Kirsty shivered. It was chilly, damp, autumnal. Summer was well and truly over, she thought, as she fastened her jacket. On Wednesday she'd be back at school. This was the last weekend of the holidays and wasn't it just typical of Jamie to spoil it? It wasn't as though they'd had a lot of time together. Jamie had been away for the first two weeks, her for the second two and, when she'd got back, Jamie hadn't seemed so keen, somehow. Had he been seeing Laura Trent? Was he with her now? Were they still in the park?

Kirsty paused by the park gates. Since the muggings, the council had installed lighting, along the path, at least. They hadn't got round to setting up the promised CCTV yet but she'd be safe enough, wouldn't she? If she kept to the path. And it would cut at least ten minutes off her walk. Speed was her motive, she told

3

herself, not spying on Jamie and Laura. Tony and Ranjit were probably making it up anyway. They were childish enough! There was probably a perfectly good reason why Jamie hadn't turned up. Nothing to do with Laura Trent.

'Just trust me, can't you?' Jamie had said last week, when he'd arrived at her house two hours late. 'I had to take the cat to the vet. Couldn't phone 'cos I was out of credit.'

'Jamie, you don't have a cat,' she'd pointed out.

'I know! But my neighbour does. And she can't manage the cat basket on her own, can she? Not with her walking frame.'

Kirsty couldn't imagine Jamie helping little old ladies somehow, with or without cats, but she'd let it go.

'Anyway, I'm here now, aren't I?' he said. 'Come on, Kirsty. Don't be mad at me. I love you. You know I do.'

He used the L-word, so readily, so easily. Was he using it now, whispering it in Laura's ear? Kirsty couldn't help looking at every park bench, every nook, every corner, as she walked along the broad path but there was no sign of Jamie or Laura. There was no sign of anybody in fact. No dog walkers, no druggies, no muggers. The park was eerily silent, deserted, its very emptiness unnerving, making her wish she'd walked the long route home. She hurried on, past the lake, round the corner, alongside the tennis courts. One more bend would bring her opposite the graffiti-sprayed toilets and beyond those, the west gate and her escape. But, before she reached the corner, she spotted something. There was something white on the grass, halfway between the path and the kiddies' play area, near a thick clump of bushes.

Plastic bag, she thought at first. White plastic bag. But no. It looked more solid, more substantial. A swan curled up, perhaps. Except it didn't really look like a swan. It looked like... Kirsty wasn't sure but there was something about it. Something about its stillness, its shape, that drew her from the path to take a closer look. The damp from the grass seeped into her shoes, making her shudder as she drew nearer. Her eyes were playing tricks. They had to be. It couldn't be what she thought it was.

Yet, with each step, her chest tightened, knowing she was right. She could see it fairly clearly now. The white tee shirt, dark jeans. The body curled in a semi-foetal position, arms slightly outstretched. A vagrant sleeping rough? But surely not in the middle of the grass like that? A drunk then, maybe, who'd fallen over? Or was it worse than that? Was she seeing the victim of a crime? A robbery. A murder!

She hurried forward, then stopped. Maybe it was some sort of trick. Was this how muggers operated? One lying on the grass, pretending to be hurt, another hiding in the bushes, waiting to pounce. Ought she to phone the police? Or was getting her phone out the worst thing she could do? Draw back, that was the answer. Get back to the path, then make the call. But it was too late. All sensible thoughts deserted her, as her eyes began to take

5

in more details of the body. Young. Male. Dark-haired.

'Jamie!' she breathed, as she darted forward.

She knelt down, touched him, gently rolled him over onto his back and screamed. It was a lad, about Jamie's age, Jamie's build, but definitely not Jamie. The front of the tee shirt was ripped and red. Red with blood. Blood on the tee shirt, on his chest, on her fingers. She crawled backwards, retching, shaking, wiping her hands on the grass, clawing at her bag, trying to open it, trying to get at her phone, trying to stand up on trembling legs that would barely support her.

He hadn't moved when she'd turned him over, hadn't opened his eyes when she'd screamed. But he was breathing. She was sure he'd been breathing. Cold to touch. But not that cold. Not deathly cold. So there was hope. If only she could get help. Press the right buttons on the phone. She managed to stand, turned towards the pathway to get some extra light, tapping frantically, making mistakes, starting again until a faint touch on her back made her drop the phone completely.

As she swung round, hands grabbed her shoulders, holding her tight and she found herself staring at the face of the boy. The dark-haired boy. The boy with blood on his chest. His face was pale but his eyes were bright, sparkling, and manic.

'Don't tell,' he hissed, as she stood there, rigid, too terrified even to shout out. 'Don't tell anyone you saw me.'

The pressure on her shoulders relaxed. He took a short step backwards.

'Don't tell,' he said again, the voice pleading this time.

He let go of her, turned and ran off across the park, his right arm held across his chest, but still Kirsty didn't move. Couldn't move. When she did, it was downwards, crumpling onto the grass, crying and shaking. She snatched up her phone and looked around. But what was she looking for? The boy coming back? Assailants, waiting to grab her bag? A passer-by to help her? She didn't know. Couldn't think. Barely knew what she was doing until she found herself back on the path, running towards the gate, out on to the street towards home. Running, like the boy had done. But how could he have run away like that? With such an injury? With all that blood? Would he get help? Go to hospital? Or did he have something to hide? His words throbbed in her aching head as she ran.

'Don't tell. Don't tell anyone you saw me.'

The light was on over the porch as Kirsty approached her house but she knew there wouldn't be anyone at home. Mum and Dad were round at her sister, Hannah's. Babysitting. She'd phone them as soon as she got in. If she got in. If she could find her key, hold it tight enough to make contact with the lock.

Once inside, she slammed the door, put the security catch on, and went round switching on all the lights, closing all the curtains. Doing all the things she wouldn't usually bother with because she still felt threatened, vulnerable, exposed, even though she was safe at home and the boy was probably miles away by now. Or was he? What if he'd turned round, followed her? What if he was watching the house?

Calm down, she told herself, grabbing a couple of painkillers out of the drawer. Stop it! Why on earth would he have followed her? He was the victim, not the criminal, for heaven's sake.

She slumped in a chair, her head aching, her heart pounding, her eyes still seeing his, intense and pleading. Who was he? Not someone from her school. Not someone local. She'd never seen him before, she was sure of that. He was the sort of person you'd remember. So where was he from? Where was he running to? What was he doing in the park? Had he been mugged? Been in a knife fight? Shot? With an air gun perhaps? Or was the wound self-inflicted? Was it as bad as it looked? It couldn't have been, could it? Not if he could run like that. Unless his flight was fuelled by fear, a rush of adrenaline.

Kirsty swallowed the tablets. It was crazy. Totally and utterly crazy. So crazy that part of her doubted it had even happened. The whole incident was beginning to feel distant, detached, surreal, impossible. But, yes, it *had* happened. It must have happened. So she ought to do something about it. Tell the police or her parents at least.

'Don't tell.'

The words held her, as she took out her mobile. Stopped her, for the moment, making her call. Why? What did he mean? Why shouldn't she tell? Who

8

shouldn't she tell? Who was he scared of? The people who'd done that to him? The police?

There'd be no point telling the police anyway, Kirsty decided. She didn't know who the boy was or what had happened. He'd frightened her, sure, but he hadn't tried to harm her. So what would she be reporting? And what were the chances of the police believing her? There was no evidence. No witnesses. They'd probably think she was mucking about. Pulling some sort of hoax. Wasting their time.

And her parents? What if she told them? Or if they came home to find her being interviewed by the police! They'd have a fit. Start fussing about what she was doing in the park on her own in the first place. They'd start droning on about trust again, insist on driving her everywhere for the rest of her life! Re-imposing all the restrictions she'd spent the last two years trying to break free of.

On the other hand, it would be nice to phone them, just to hear another voice, to break the oppressive silence of the empty house. Maybe she'd hear her nephew, Henry, screaming away in the background. Toddler tantrums, nagging parents, normality. She tapped her phone but nothing happened. No light. Nothing on the screen. Must have broken. When she dropped it. When she'd felt the cold hand touching her back.

She shuddered, wondering whether she had the energy to cross the room to the house phone. Its sudden ring decided her. She got up, lifted the receiver.

'Hello?' she said quietly, as if expecting another shock.

'Hi, Kirsty.'

'Jamie! Where the hell have you been?' she said, bursting into tears.

'Hey, Kirsty,' he said. 'Don't cry! I'm sorry. I've been trying to phone your mobile for ages. Kirsty, what's wrong? What is it?'

'Nothing!' she snapped, slamming down the receiver. 'Nothing you'd care about!'

She phoned him back. Immediately. She always did. It was pathetic, she knew, but there was something about Jamie Sullivan she couldn't resist. No, not something, everything! The casual good looks, the cheeky smile, his crazy humour, the way he kissed, the way he bounced into a room. Everything! Trouble was, half the girls in their school couldn't resist him either and he knew it.

She'd refused the first few times he'd asked her out, knowing his reputation, but eventually she'd given in and now she was hooked. Now, for better or for worse, she was Jamie Sullivan's official girlfriend and if he wanted to believe her crying was tears of disappointment because he'd stood her up again, then let him. She didn't mention the trouble in the park. Somehow, she didn't want to, she didn't think Jamie would understand.

'Sorry about missing the film,' Jamie said. 'I bumped into Laura.'

Staggeringly honest by Jamie's standards. Did this mean the end? Was he about to announce that he and luscious Laura were back together?

10

'Tony and Ranjit might have told you.'

Meaning he knew for sure that they had and was about to launch into an implausible explanation.

'They probably told you how upset she was?' he said, more hesitantly. 'About her granddad dying?'

'No.'

'Yeah, well she was. 'Cos they were like really close. She just wanted to talk about it, you know? And, by the time I'd walked her home and realised what time it was, I couldn't get an answer from your phone or anything. I mean, you don't need to worry about Laura and me. You know that, don't you? It's over, completely over. But, well, I couldn't just tell her to piss off, could I? Not when she was so upset.'

'Was this the same granddad who died last month?' Kirsty couldn't resist asking.

'No,' said Jamie, without a pause. 'Her other one. That's what made it so upsetting, see? Losing two in such a short space of time.'

Kirsty was fairly confident that both Laura's grandfathers were perfectly healthy and living happy, active lives somewhere but she didn't want to argue with Jamie anymore. She was too exhausted, so she let him rattle on about how much he loved her, how they'd spend the remaining three days of the holiday together and how she could help him with all the holiday homework he hadn't got round to doing. Mention of homework led him onto an impersonation of their form tutor, Mr Lane, which made her laugh so much that she almost forgot

11

about her ruined date and the trauma in the park.

Only when the phone call ended, did it all come back. The image of the blood soaked tee shirt, the desperation in the boy's eyes, in his voice. He'd be all right, she told herself. The boy would be all right. Apart from the injury, he'd looked clean, well dressed, from what she could tell. He must have a home, somewhere. He must live with someone. Someone who'd make sure he got medical help. It wasn't her responsibility. She didn't need to do anything. There was nothing she *could* do.

She phoned her parents, still unsure about whether to tell them.

'Kirsty, you'll never guess what?' were her mother's first words. 'I got Henry to use his potty!'

'Mum,' Kirsty began.

'Hannah says he won't go near it,' her mother rattled on. 'But he's just used it for Granny, haven't you my clever, clever boy. He did a great big...'

Kirsty held the phone away from her ear. Her problem, if she decided to tell them, would have to wait. No matter how important it turned out to be, it simply couldn't compete with young Henry's bowels.

Chapter 2

Late on Monday afternoon, Simon stood looking down onto the street. It was happening again. This feeling, this weird feeling that someone was watching him. His heavy bursts of breath steamed up the bedroom window, obscuring his view. He wiped it with his sleeve. Peered out again. There were several people hurrying past but none of them looked up; no one seemed interested in him. Yet he'd been so sure, as he walked home through town that someone was following.

Could it have been Luke? Luke had been hanging round town earlier, so maybe he'd followed him, at a distance. Mucking about. Trying to wind him up. It was possible. Luke was crazy enough for anything.

A sharp knock on the door made Simon swing round.

'Yeah,' he said, as the door opened.

'You're back,' said Jaz.

'Looks like it.'

'Can I come in?'

As she was in already, with the door firmly closed behind her, there seemed little point objecting.

'So where've you been?' said Jaz. 'Anywhere interesting?'

Her tone was light, encouraging but Simon wasn't

13

fooled. No way was he going to tell her where he'd been. He wasn't going to tell anyone yet.

'Just town,' he said.

'I wanted to talk to you anyway,' said Jaz, sitting on the edge of Simon's bed, tracing over the burn marks on his duvet with her finger. 'About these.'

Simon stared at her but said nothing.

'How did they get there?' she asked.

'How do you think?' said Simon.

'I expect you were playing with a cigarette lighter,' said Jaz, calmly.

'Yeah, whatever.'

'And I expect you did it sometime yesterday, after your Auntie Roz had been.'

'Yeah, well, she pisses me off, all right?'

'Do you want to sit down?' Jaz asked.

'No. I don't want to sit down and I don't want to talk about it, OK?'

Simon carried on staring at Jaz, hoping to freeze her out, make her go away, yet knowing it wouldn't work. She was one of the younger care workers, the ones who wore jeans, tee shirts, trainers, studs in their eyebrows and navels. Trying to be cool, trying to make out like they understood. Well, they didn't. They didn't understand shit.

'Roz doesn't mean to upset you,' Jaz was saying. 'She loves you.'

'Oh sure!' said Simon. 'So that's why she dumped me here, is it? Because she loves me?'

14

He sat down in the armchair in the corner of the room, not because he wanted to sit, certainly not because he wanted to talk, but because he knew the rules. The unwritten rules. Talk to Jaz now, pretend to listen, pretend to conform, or face the heavy brigade later. The supervisor. The psychologist.

'She didn't dump you,' Jaz said, quietly. 'And there's nothing to say you won't be able to go back if...'

'If I'm a good boy?'

'Something like that,' said Jaz, smiling. 'Not setting fire to your bedroom would be a good start.'

'It won't make no difference,' said Simon, shrugging. 'They won't have me back. Whatever I do.'

'That's not true,' said Jaz. 'Paul's really keen to have you back and Roz isn't totally set against it. She's just worried about Ben and Ellie.'

'Yeah, well she would be, wouldn't she?' said Simon. 'They're her real kids, aren't they? And besides it's all a load of rubbish, innit? An excuse! It wasn't me that gave Ben that dope. He got it off his mates at school. Idiot didn't even try it! And, as for Ellie, it's not me that freaks her, is it? It's them. Paul and Roz. Screaming and yelling all the time.'

'Yes,' said Jaz. 'But who are they screaming and yelling at? I know they don't always handle things well; they'd be the first to admit it. That's why they feel they need a break, a cooling-off period, for all of you. It doesn't mean they don't love you. It's just...'

'Just my behaviour they don't like, right?' said

15

Simon. 'I know. I've heard it all before. I stay out too late. I'm aggressive. I'm a bad influence on Ben. I tell lies. It's making Roz ill. Well it's them that's lying. It's nothing to do with any of that. It's 'cos I went to see...'

He paused as his bedroom door was thrown open and a girl burst in.

'Briony!' said Jaz. 'Can't you knock?'

'You gotta come,' Briony squealed. 'Quick. Dave wants you. It's Luke! He's slashin' all the furniture in the lounge. He's got a knife!'

Jaz leapt up and raced out of the room, followed by Briony. Through the open door, Simon could hear the excited shrieks of other kids, the stamp of feet running around. Care home! It was more like a bloody zoo. One of those old-fashioned zoos with tiny cages full of pacing tigers, psychotic baboons and depressed bears pulling their own fur out in matted, flea-ridden clumps.

Were all care homes as bad as this? Full of loonies like Luke, rampaging round with knives? Probably not. This one was for special cases. Kids with 'behavioural problems'. Nobody had spelt it out for him but he wasn't stupid. It was pretty obvious.

He already knew a fair amount about the other inmates, even though he'd only been here a month. He'd tried to keep himself to himself but it wasn't easy, especially with Briony, who never stopped asking questions, and Luke who seemed to see him as some sort of threat or challenge. Constantly hovering, staring at him, trying to pick arguments. Then, at the other extreme, was little

16

Ricky, who cowered in corners, sucking a piece of cloth, never saying a word to anybody.

Even without getting involved, Simon had learnt enough to realise that the care home wasn't an orphanage. All the kids had families somewhere. Families who didn't want them, couldn't cope with them, couldn't look after them, even deliberately harmed them, in some cases. So was it surprising that some of the inmates cut themselves, refused to speak or ran amok with knives?

Well, he wasn't going to end up like that! He was perfectly sane, thank you very much, and intended to stay that way. He got up, slammed the bedroom door, shutting out all the noise, before bending down and pulling a carrier bag out from under the bed, where he'd shoved it yesterday after Roz had gone. She always brought him a present, every Sunday afternoon when she came to visit. He never showed any interest, never opened them while she was there but he opened them all eventually. Usually when he needed something to sell so he could buy cigarettes or a bit of dope.

Not that anyone would want to buy this week's offering, he thought, tipping the contents of the bag onto the floor. Two white shirts, a pair of grey trousers, a green jumper and a striped tie. His new school uniform. Lovely!

His old school hadn't had a uniform but he couldn't go there anymore because it was on the other side of town, near Roz's house, too far to travel. It was a dump anyway and they didn't exactly want him back, did they? Not after that business at the end of term, when he'd had a go at that prat of a Deputy Head. Moving had saved them the trouble of excluding him.

So now he had to start Year 11 at Whitecroft, a posh school that called itself an Academy and reluctantly took in kids from the care home because they had to, because they'd got some sort of arrangement with them. Well, they needn't bother taking him! Simon picked up a cup of cold coffee off the bedside table and poured it slowly over the shirts, the jumper, the trousers, the tie. He watched the brown liquid soaking into the clothes, then smiled as he shoved them all back in the carrier bag. That should delay things for a while.

'What do you mean?' Dave asked, on Wednesday morning. 'You haven't got a uniform?'

Simon pulled the duvet up to his chin and lay, staring at the ceiling. He couldn't be bothered with any of this. He was knackered. He'd been awake since four o'clock, unable to get back to sleep after the nightmare. The same nightmare he always had. The one about his mum. The nightmare that was really a memory. The one he couldn't shake off.

'Where is it?' Dave was saying. 'The stuff your auntie brought?'

Simon turned his head, lowering his eyes towards the floor by way of an answer. Dave tipped the uniform out of the bag, scowling as he saw the dried-on stains.

'I'll get some from the box,' Dave said, rubbing his hand across his bald head, as if trying to polish it, as if it wasn't shiny enough already. 'There's bound to be something your size.'

'Don't bother,' Simon shouted after him. ''Cos I'm not going.'

It was Jaz who brought the clothes back. Jaz, with her smooth, dark skin and even smoother voice.

'Come on, Simon,' she said. 'You know you have to go.'

'Why? What's the point? I'll probably get kicked out by the end of the week.'

'It doesn't have to be like that,' Jaz said. 'You're a bright lad.'

'Been reading my records, have you?'

'Every night,' she said, laughing. 'They're better than a novel. But I don't need your records to tell me you're bright. I only have to talk to you.'

'Give it a rest,' said Simon, blushing.

Jaz often had this effect on him. And worse besides. She was gorgeous. Really stunning, like she ought to be a model or something. Only looked about eighteen but was actually twenty-six. Way too old, way out of his league. And her interest in him was totally proper, totally professional.

'All right,' he said, beginning to feel uncomfortable, as her dark eyes rested on him. 'I'll get dressed. If you leave me alone.'

'That's my boy,' she said, winking at him as she left.

19

They didn't have mirrors in the bedrooms, in case people decided to break them and cut themselves, Simon supposed. Not that he needed a mirror this morning. He knew he looked a total eejit in a shirt and tie, he didn't need confirmation. The clothes Jaz had brought were better than the new stuff from Roz. They were worn, creased, scruffy but he hated uniform of any sort, hated looking like everyone else. Because he wasn't like everyone else, was he? He took off the jumper and tie, stuffed them into his bag, left his shirt hanging loose outside his trousers and put on his trainers. No way was he wearing black shoes. No way at all.

His irritation made him careless. As he left the bedroom, he bumped into Luke. Literally. Big, big mistake. Before Simon could even think about apologising, Luke had pinned him up against the wall, almost crushing his chest, squeezing the breath out of his lungs. They were about the same age but Luke was bigger, heavier, stronger.

Simon tried to speak but Luke wasn't listening. He'd completely lost it, shouting, swearing, banging Simon's head against the wall. Well, if he wanted a fight he could have one. Simon summoned what little energy he had left and brought his knee up sharp into Luke's groin. As Luke crumpled, Simon threw himself on top of him, intending to hold him down but Luke wasn't giving up that easily, not now they had an audience of people rushing out of bedrooms, gathering round, shrieking, squealing, yelling.

Luke's head shot forward, cracking the bridge of Simon's nose, making him feel sick, faint, forcing him, momentarily, to close his eyes and, when he opened them, it was to see gushes of blood, *his* blood, spurting from his nose onto Luke's school shirt. Simon rolled away, scrambled up, pushed past a couple of people and stood with his back against the wall, shaking, involuntary tears streaming down his face.

'Wimp!' Luke yelled, leaping up, launching himself at Simon.

Simon's fist clenched, lashed out before he knew what he was doing and smacked hard into Luke's face, sending him crashing to the floor, where he lay, totally still, silencing the crowd. The crowd but not the voice in Simon's head. Uncle Paul's voice, deep, disapproving.

'I've told you, Simon. You're gonna turn out just like your dad, you are. If you go on like this.'

Was he? Was Paul right? Was that what was happening to him?

'What the hell's going on?'

A real voice this time. Dave's voice. Dave's muscular, tattooed arms parting the crowd and behind Dave, Jaz and several other workers, some moving forward, fussing over Luke, others leading Simon away, back to his room.

'I saw it!' Briony was squealing, her red and black streaked hair flopping round her face as she spoke. 'Luke started it. It was Luke's fault.'

Briony couldn't have seen it, Simon was sure. Not the

21

start of it. So why did she get involved? Because she liked him? Possibly. She was always hanging around but he'd hardly encouraged her. Not in that way. Sure he talked to her more than he talked to the others. You had to talk to someone, didn't you? But he'd never come on to her. She wasn't his type. She was fifteen but looked and acted about twelve. All sort of giggly and squealy. No figure at all, with limbs so thin they looked as though they might snap if you brushed past her.

He'd heard Luke teasing her about her weight, telling her she was fat and ugly, whenever staff weren't around, so maybe this was Briony getting her own back, stitching Luke up. It didn't really matter. What mattered was that she stuck to her story, made it sound convincing and near enough to Simon's version to get him off the hook. At least, in part.

There'd be an enquiry, case conference or something. Another round of meetings, discussions, therapy sessions. Anger management. Dealing with aggression. Counting to ten. Punching pillows instead of faces. All very well, until someone had you up against a wall and you didn't happen to have your pillow with you. On the bright side, at least it got him out of going to school. In the short term, anyway. Luke, the doctor said, shouldn't go back until Monday. Simon, much to his annoyance, was passed fit almost immediately and, by midday, considered settled enough, stable enough, to go in for the afternoon.

'Give it a chance,' Jaz whispered, as she delivered

him to the Head of Year. 'Just give it a chance. You never know, you might like it.'

'Who's dead now?' Kirsty asked Jamie, as he sat beside her for afternoon registration.

'What do you mean?'

'I saw you, Jamie! With Laura. Outside the music room. So which one of her unfortunate relatives has passed away this time?'

'Oh, no one. No. It was nothing like that. She needed help sorting out her timetable. She's in the same sets as me for most things.'

Kirsty scowled. She didn't need reminding that Laura and Jamie were together for most subjects. She was only grateful that Laura was in a different tutor group.

'And you had to put your arm round her, I suppose?' she asked.

'Kirsty Broughton,' Mr Lane shouted. 'Do you think you could possibly keep your love life out of tutor time and just answer the register?'

'Yes, Sir, sorry, Sir,' Kirsty muttered, as the class sniggered. 'Well, did you?' she hissed at Jamie.

'Did I what?'

'Have to put your arm round her? And stick your tongue down her ear!'

'Ugh,' said Mr Lane, as Kirsty realised she'd raised her voice again. 'No tongues, Kirsty. Please no tongues.'

Kirsty put her head down to cover her blushes, to stop her having to look at Jamie who was laughing, enjoying every minute. So she was only vaguely aware of the Head of Year coming in and introducing the new boy, Simon Wells.

'My tongue was nowhere near Laura's ear,' Jamie said, catching hold of Kirsty's hand as she stood up in response to the bell.

'Jamie,' said Mr Lane. 'Spare a moment from your tangled love life, will you and take Simon to his maths lesson. Room 15.'

Jamie let go of Kirsty's hand. They both paused by the teacher's desk and looked at Simon. Jamie's glance was brief, uninterested but Kirsty stared. Continued to stare. At the boy's face, at his intensely blue eyes and the bruise around the top of his nose. The bruise that hadn't been there before. He stared back, unresponsive, for a second, then it came. A half smile, that might have been a sneer or a flicker of recognition. The confirmation she'd been waiting for. It was him. It was definitely him. The boy from the park.

She watched him turn, walk out of the classroom, following Jamie along the corridor. The two of them so similar: tall, same slim build, dark brown hair. It was only in the detail they were different. Simon's hair was a little shorter, straighter, his eyes were blue, not brown, and his face was more sharply defined, harder, less cherubic than Jamie's. But it was easy to see how she could have been mistaken, at first, in the park.

At least the boy was OK. Well enough to come to school. She'd thought about him a lot since Saturday, looked out for him, as she'd travelled to Jamie's or into town to buy a new phone and even checked the local paper to see if any teenage lads had been reported missing. They hadn't but she'd wondered whether she'd done the right thing, keeping the incident to herself. Heard his bizarre words over and over in her head.

'Don't tell. Don't tell anyone you saw me.'

Well now he was here, in her school, in her class. Now, at least, she'd have a chance to find out what had happened, what he'd meant.

Chapter 3

Kirsty didn't see Simon again that day. He wasn't in any of her lessons and wasn't around at the end of the afternoon. She saw him several times on Thursday but he never came close enough for her to speak to. Was he deliberately avoiding her?

'What you looking at him for?' Jamie asked, during morning registration on Friday. 'Fancy him, do you?'

'Might do,' Kirsty had said, on the grounds that it wouldn't do Jamie any harm to think he had a rival.

'Not your type,' said Jamie, dismissively. 'Bit of a bad lad, from what I hear. He's at Oakfields.'

'So?' said Kirsty. 'It's a care home not a flaming remand centre. It doesn't mean he's a bad lad, as you put it.'

'No,' said Jamie, 'but he's already had a go at Luke. You know, Luke Harris, 11G?'

'That great ape!' said Kirsty. 'He's twice Simon's size. I'm sure he can look after himself.'

'And,' said Jamie, 'Simon got chucked out of history yesterday for swearing at Mrs O'Brien. I mean, you'd have to be a bit of a nutter to try it on with her, wouldn't you?'

Nutter or not, Kirsty was determined to talk to Simon and finally tracked him down at lunchtime. He was on his own, behind the art block. He threw down a rolled-up cigarette as she approached and swung round to face her.

'What you doing creeping up, like that? I thought you were a teacher!'

'Sorry,' said Kirsty. 'I wasn't creeping. I came to talk to you.'

'Yeah, well, you shouldn't have bothered,' said Simon, starting to move off.

'Hey, wait a minute,' said Kirsty. 'You could at least tell me what happened.'

'Some idiot head-butted me,' said Simon, rubbing the bruise on his nose.

'Not that,' said Kirsty. 'You know what I mean. In the park.'

'What park?' said Simon.

'Don't play games,' said Kirsty. 'In the park on Saturday night! We both know it was you. Look, I won't tell. I haven't. I haven't told anyone. I just want to know what happened.'

'Yeah, well I'd love to tell you,' said Simon, 'but I haven't the faintest clue what you're on about.'

Kirsty hadn't known what to expect when she'd started the conversation but it certainly wasn't this. Absolute denial. She stared at Simon's face, at those eyes. Could she have been mistaken? In the dark and with the shock and everything. But no. It was the same boy, she was sure of it.

'Just tell me whether you got it sorted,' she said, transferring her gaze to his chest. 'Did you see a doctor?'

'It's not me that needs a doctor,' he said, pointedly.

'You were covered in blood!' Kirsty insisted. 'Your chest was covered in blood, like you'd been stabbed or something.'

Simon looked at her, smiled, pulled off the tie that was hanging loosely round his neck and started slowly unbuttoning his shirt.

'Does it look like I've been stabbed anytime recently?' he asked, holding his shirt open.

It didn't. There wasn't a mark on him. No plaster, no bandage, no gash, wound or bruise. Not even a scratch as far as Kirsty could see. How could he have healed so quickly? It was so bizarre, so unbelievable that Kirsty couldn't resist checking. She stretched out her hand, letting her fingers trace down his chest, feeling for scars but finding nothing but perfectly smooth skin and fine, dark hair.

'Nice!' said Simon, putting his hands over hers.

Kirsty tried to pull away but he was holding her too tightly. He'd got the wrong idea entirely. He thought she was coming on to him! His head was leaning forward, his lips almost touching hers and the worst thing was, she wasn't doing or saying anything to stop him.

'Not interrupting anything, am I?'

The grip loosened, Kirsty pulled away, turned to see Jamie scowling at them.

'Yeah,' said Simon.

'No!' said Kirsty, following Jamie, as he stormed off. 'It's not what you think.'

Mercifully Simon wasn't in any of Kirsty's sets, so she didn't have to face him again on Friday or have much contact with him over the next week. During registration times, she kept well away, too embarrassed to even look at him but that didn't mean she didn't think about him. In fact, she thought about little else. Trying to work it out, trying to find some logical explanation. Simon was definitely the boy in the park unless he had a clone or twin brother, which seemed a touch unlikely. He'd been covered in blood but was clearly uninjured. So either the blood wasn't real or...it was someone else's blood. Luke's blood? Is that where the fight with Luke had taken place? In the park?

It didn't take her long to find out that she was on the wrong track with that one. So had Simon attacked someone else? Did he make a habit of it? Was that why he'd urged her not to tell? Because he'd committed a crime. Hurt someone. Killed someone! Could there have been a body hidden in those bushes? Had she, unwittingly, been an accessory to a murder? Ought she to tell someone? Or was she simply letting her imagination run wild?

She hadn't even told Jamie. Not even after the playground incident.

'He'd just been stung by a wasp,' she'd said in response to Jamie's questioning about Simon's open shirt. 'He asked me to look at it.'

Jamie hadn't believed her but he'd been remarkably attentive since and had barely glanced at Laura Trent. So

29

not all bad news and, by the end of the week, Kirsty's fears about Simon were starting to settle. There had been no police reports about bodies under bushes in the park, no rumours about gangs or knife fights, no more muggings. She still didn't have an explanation but whatever Simon had been up to he couldn't have hurt anybody, could he?

At twenty past two on Sunday afternoon Simon switched off his TV and lay waiting for the sound of Roz's old Ford Escort pulling up outside but all he could hear was the rain gushing from the broken gutter, splattering onto the window. It had been raining all day, absolutely bucketing down, so maybe she wouldn't bother. Would he care if she didn't? He wasn't really sure. Not that it mattered. He was fairly confident Roz *would* turn up whatever the weather. She was like that, Roz. Always did what she said she was going to do.

'Your mum would have wanted me to look after you,' Roz had told him all those years ago. 'And I will. You know that don't you, Simon?'

Well, she'd kept her word. Fed him, clothed him, 'tried to get him sorted out', as she'd put it. Until a few months back, when he'd broken his part of the deal, big time, when it had all got too much for her. He reached into his pocket, without really thinking about what he was doing, and pulled out the black leather wallet Roz had bought him. One of the few presents he hadn't lost or sold. He opened it and took out a picture of his mum.

The picture he'd carried around since she died but rarely looked at.

He looked now, trying to connect the person in the photograph with his memories, trying to bring to life the smiling face that stared back at him but it was all wrong. This wasn't how he remembered her. Sure the blonde hair was right, falling straight and loose on her shoulders, dark roots showing. The eyes, wide and blue, slightly paler than his own. But the problem was . . . the problem was, he only really had one memory of his mum. A memory he didn't want to have. A memory he was trying to replace. Trying to paste the photograph over it. Trying to remember the good times, the happy times, if there'd ever been any.

He was still examining the picture when he heard the car draw up. He put the photo on the bedside table, stood up and glanced out of the window to see Roz waving at him as she got out of the car and waddled towards the door. There was never any point looking for traces of his mum in Roz. They were as different as sisters could be. Roz was small, quite plump, with naturally frizzy, mousy hair and greyish narrow eyes and, though she was two years younger than his mum, she'd always been the sensible one, the mature one, as she constantly reminded him.

'Hi, Simon,' she said, bursting into his room without knocking, like she used to do at home.

He dodged as she bustled towards him, arms outstretched. Part of him had looked forward to the visit but now she was here, everything she did annoyed him. It was all so false. The smile, the eager look in her eyes. As if she wanted to see him, as though she actually wanted to be here.

'Too big for hugs?' she said, flopping down into the armchair. 'Never mind.'

She reached into her pockets, unloading paper bags onto the table.

'I've brought you some chocolate,' she said. 'And some more pens and stuff for school. How's it going?'

Simon shrugged but didn't answer.

'Made any new friends?'

'No.'

How long would this go on? The polite, tense questions, his monosyllabic answers. How long before the fixed smile faded and Roz got onto the things she really wanted to say? Simon looked down, picking his nails, as Roz rattled through the weather, how busy Paul was with his plumbing jobs and what Ben and Ellie had been up to. Painting a picture of how cosy and normal life was ... without Simon around. Not that she actually said that but her meaning was clear enough.

'Jaz tells me there's been a bit of trouble,' Roz said at last. 'Want to talk about it?'

'No point if Jaz has already told you,' said Simon.

'Paul's worried about you,' said Roz.

Simon felt his shoulders stiffen. Those words always signalled trouble. Roz always quoted Paul if there was something unpleasant to say.

'He thinks you've been worse since ... '

'It's got nothing to do with that! If I've been worse it's because of this bloody dump.'

'Simon, you know that's not true,' said Roz, putting on the hurt voice that made him cringe. 'You started kicking off again way before you came here. Paul's right. He said it would lead to trouble if you saw *him*.'

'Listen,' said Simon. 'If that's what you want to believe, fine. But you can't stop me. It's my life. You can't stop me seeing my own dad!'

'But after everything we said,' Roz went on. 'After everything he's done to you. I can't believe you'd even *want* to see him.'

'Yeah, right, and that's what you've always told him, isn't it? Not to bother writing. Not to bother phoning. Because I was better off without him. Because I didn't want to know. But I did! I need to try and get my head round it. All of it.'

'All what?' said Roz, genuinely confused.

'The truth.'

'The truth!' said Roz. 'And you think you'll get that from him, do you? Well, you won't! All you'll get from him is lies. He'll lie to you like he lied to everyone else. He'll tie you up in so many knots you won't know what to believe.'

'At least I can listen,' said Simon. 'At least I can give him a chance, which is more than anyone else ever did.'

Simon paused, looking at Roz's bewildered face.

'You don't understand, do you?' he said. 'I have to! It's my fault he's . . . '

'I might have known!' said Roz. 'Is that what he's been telling you? That it was your fault? That's typical of him, that is. Deny everything. Put the blame on someone else! Even if it's his own kid.'

'No!' said Simon. 'He didn't say anything. He didn't need to. I don't need anybody to tell me, do I?'

Simon closed his eyes, screwed them up tight, trying to squeeze away the pictures, the pain, the sickness that rushed at him, all at once. Squeezing them into a tight black ball that fought back, trying to expand, like a black hole, sucking him in.

'It wasn't your fault,' said Roz, quietly. 'None of it was your fault, Simon.'

Simon's eyes snapped open but the blackness was still there.

'You don't get it, do you?' Simon said, knowing he had to get out, escape before the blackness took over completely, before he did something stupid. 'You just don't get it.'

He grabbed his jacket, heading towards the door.

'Simon, wait!' Roz said, struggling to pull herself from the chair. 'Where are you going?'

'Out!' he said, slamming the door behind him.

Kirsty was so keen to avoid looking at Simon that she didn't even realise he was missing on Monday morning, until Mr Lane reached the end of the register.

'Simon Wells?' he repeated, his sharp eyes scanning the classroom. 'Anybody know where he is?'

Nobody did but it didn't take them long to find out. At break Briony Phillips was telling anyone who would listen.

'He's done a bunk,' she was informing her group of Year 10 friends, as Kirsty edged closer. 'Took off on Sunday afternoon and didn't come back. Police have been out looking for him and asking questions at Oakfields and everything.'

'The police?' Kirsty couldn't help saying. 'Why?'

Briony folded her arms defensively, defiantly.

'Who are you?' she asked. 'What's it got to do with you?'

'I'm in Simon's class. I'm a friend,' Kirsty lied.

'Oh,' said Briony, flatly. 'Well, Oakfields have to call the cops, don't they? If one of us goes missing. 'Cos if they don't and anything happens, then they're like responsible, aren't they?'

'I suppose so,' said Kirsty vacantly. 'So why did he go? What happened?' she added, not knowing why she'd asked or why it felt important to know.

'Dunno,' said Briony. 'I mean he's always going off on his own and stuff. For hours and hours sometimes. But he's never stayed out all night before. Not since he's been at Oakfields anyway. I'm a bit worried about him. He's ...'

'Attention-seeking,' Jamie whispered to Kirsty, putting his arm round her waist, steering her away. 'That's what he's doing. Hiding out somewhere, I expect. Winding everyone up.'

35

'Do you mind?' said Kirsty, shaking him off. 'I was talking to Briony.'

'You won't get much sense out of her,' said Jamie. 'She's a nutter. Has to go to the medical room everyday for her lunch.'

'She's got an eating disorder, Jamie,' Kirsty snapped. 'That doesn't make her a nutter.'

'It does in my book.'

'And which book is that, Jamie? How to be a thoughtless prat in five easy lessons?'

'Ooooh,' said Jamie, laughing. 'No need to get nasty just because your friend Simon's disappeared.'

'He's hardly a friend,' said Kirsty.

'So why all the interest?'

'Because he's missing, that's all. Because anything could have happened to him. It's called caring, Jamie. Caring about other people. Not your strong suit, I know.'

'What the hell's wrong with you, today?' he snapped, before storming off.

Kirsty wasn't sure. She had no idea why she'd been sniping at Jamie or why her head was so full of Simon Wells. Why she couldn't get over that bizarre business in the park. It was bad enough before but now...now he was missing. What if the incident in the park was somehow connected to his disappearance? What if he was in trouble? Real trouble, that she'd been covering up?

Should she tell someone? Should she tell what little she knew? And if she did? Wouldn't they think it odd that she hadn't said anything earlier? At the time. When it happened. How was she supposed to explain that? When she didn't even know herself.

'You're not going out with him or anything, are you?'

'What?' said Kirsty, surprised by Briony's sudden reappearance. 'Jamie? Yes, I am. Sort of.'

'Jamie not Simon?' said Briony.

'Simon? No. Not Simon!'

'Good,' said Briony, turning to walk away.

'Er, you were going to tell me something, though,' said Kirsty. 'About Simon. Before. When Jamie turned up.'

'It was just something Simon told me the other day,' said Briony. 'He came in all sort of panicky. Reckoned someone was watching him. Following him.'

'Who?' said Kirsty.

'He didn't know. Said it was just a feeling.'

'Did he tell anyone else? Have *you* told anyone? The police? The care staff?'

'Yeah,' said Briony. 'But I don't think they took much notice. No one ever listens to what I say. Besides, they think Simon's a bit . . . you know . . . paranoid. After what happened and everything. With his mum. I mean I know it was a long time ago but—'

'Kirsty Broughton! Briony Phillips!' a sharp, female voice yelled across the playground. 'The bell went five minutes ago. Get to your lessons. Now!'

'It's probably nothing anyway,' said Briony, as they split up. 'He's probably just gone walkabout again. He'll turn up. Won't he?'

37

Chapter 4

Simon sat in the office at Oakfields with two of the care workers who'd pounced on him the minute he'd walked in, bombarding him with questions. Questions he couldn't answer. Questions he didn't want to answer.

'I'm back, all right,' he said. 'So what's the problem?'

'The problem,' said Al, 'is that you can't just disappear whenever you feel like it, bunk off school, then turn up and behave as though nothing's happened.'

'Can't I?' said Simon, standing up. 'So what you gonna do about it?'

He stormed out of the office and ran upstairs. There was no one around, no one to bump into. It was only three o'clock so all the inmates were still at school and there were only two people on duty. That's why he'd chosen this time, hoping to sneak in without anyone noticing but he'd reckoned without Al's personal radar. Well it didn't matter. They couldn't force him to say anything. Not if he didn't want to. What could they do to him? Throw him out?

He bolted into his room and slammed the door. He couldn't lock it, of course, privacy wasn't allowed, so he did the next best thing, pulling the chest of drawers away from the wall, wedging it up against the door. He threw himself on the bed; lay waiting for the footsteps, the knock, the plea for entry but it didn't come.

Cooling-off period. That was the jargon, wasn't it? They were giving him time to settle, to calm down, decide to be sensible, make a full confession about where he'd been, what he'd been up to. Only he couldn't, could he? Because he barely knew. Because the black hole that had opened up on Sunday had just kept growing, swallowing him up until he didn't know where he was or who he was.

He'd been wandering round town when it started to fade, with no idea of how he'd got there or how long he'd been there. The only clue was the shirt; the damp sticky tee shirt he'd found screwed up in his jacket pocket. He'd dumped the shirt in a bin behind one of the shops, without looking at it. Without really wanting to look. But it was no good. He knew what it meant and now that the blackness had gone completely, he remembered. He remembered exactly where he'd been and what he'd done.

Was this how it started? The madness. Was this what had happened to his dad? Doing stuff you didn't want to do. Hardly knowing you were doing it. Barely remembering afterwards. Not wanting to remember. So perhaps, in the end, you didn't. Maybe one day the black hole swallowed you and never spat you out. Maybe that's why his dad...

Simon leapt off the bed, went over to the chest of drawers, opened the middle one, threw out all the socks, underpants, debris and found what he was looking for right at the bottom. He took out the large, brown envelope, went back to the bed, sat down and pulled out the pile of newspaper cuttings. The ones from the local paper, the national papers. The ones from almost ten years ago.

They weren't his. He'd been too young, at the time, to read newspapers or know which articles to cut out. These belonged to Roz. He'd found them a few months back, at the same time he'd found the letter. When Roz had demanded them back, he'd told her he'd torn them up, thrown them away. She hadn't believed him, of course. She never did but he'd kept the documents well hidden so she couldn't prove anything. Couldn't take them away from him.

He spread them out on the bed. They looked old, faded, discoloured, like his memories, but the print was clear enough to read. Horribly, painfully clear.

'Everything OK?' Kirsty's dad asked, as he walked in the kitchen.

'Yeah,' said Kirsty, looking up from her homework. 'Mum phoned to say she'd be late so I've shoved that casserole in the oven.'

'Good girl,' said her dad, throwing the evening paper onto the table. 'I'll finish it all off. How was school?'

'Fine,' said Kirsty, guessing her dad meant the lessons and wouldn't be interested in the row she'd had with Jamie or the rumours about Simon Wells that had been flying round school by the end of the day.

Oakfields, apparently, had phoned the school to say that Simon was back. According to Briony his auntie had brought him back but according to Luke, the police had picked Simon up in town.

'No, he just went back on his own,' someone else had said.

Impossible to know what was true, Kirsty thought, as she finished highlighting her history notes but whatever the truth was, it had nothing to do with her. He was back now, safe, saving her the trouble of making a decision. She didn't have to say anything or do anything. If she had any sense, she'd just forget all about it and stay well away from him.

'I'm just going up to get changed,' said her dad.

'OK,' said Kirsty, vacantly. 'I'll set the table.'

She put her books in her bag, set out three mats and picked up the evening paper from where Dad had dumped it. She winced as she saw the picture on the front. A picture of an elderly woman, her face bruised, cut, swollen. Another mugging? It was unbelievable. How anyone could do something like that to an old lady. But no. It wasn't an attack. Not as such. The woman had fallen. After something had frightened her. When she was walking the few yards home from her friend's house. On Sunday evening. The evening Simon Wells had gone missing.

The paper started to tremble in Kirsty's hands as she read the details. How the woman had gone down the alleyway at the back of her house, how she'd found the dead body, covered in blood. Only it wasn't dead, was it?

'Terrible, isn't it?'

'What?' said Kirsty, dropping the paper as her dad came back in.

'About that poor woman,' said her dad, picking the paper up. 'Is that what you were reading?'

'No! I mean, yes. Sort of. Just saw the picture.'

'Some yob playing a practical joke, they reckon,' said her dad. 'Pretending to be dead, then leaping up. Frightened her half to death.'

'Does it give a description?' said Kirsty, quietly. 'Does it say who did it?'

'Teenage lad,' said her dad. 'Dark-haired. That's all. I think she was too shocked to remember much.'

'Did he say anything?'

'Who? The lad? No I don't think so. Doesn't mention anything. Why? Are you OK, Kirsty? You look a bit pale.'

'Dad, I . . .'

She was on the verge of blurting it out. Saying she knew who it was. But did she? Could it be coincidence? And, even if it was Simon, did she really want to get involved? Have to answer all the questions it was sure to throw up?

'Er, I think I'm just hungry,' she said.

She picked up her bag, took it to her room and sat on her bed, thinking about the woman, unable to shake away the image of split lips, eyes forced shut by the swelling, a face so distorted it was barely a face at all. What was she supposed to do? Making wild accusations wouldn't get her anywhere. Simon would only deny it, wouldn't he? And what proof did she have?

So what were the alternatives? Keep quiet again? Let him get away with it? Let him keep doing it? Let him keep playing his sick, perverted, little joke until someone else got hurt? If it was a joke. He hadn't stolen anything from her or the woman but maybe he'd intended to. Lost his nerve at the last minute? A mugging gone wrong? It didn't seem likely but then neither did anything else.

She pushed her bag onto the floor and stood up. There was no point telling herself not to get involved, she was already involved. No point telling herself to keep away from Simon because she knew she wasn't going to. She was going to talk to him again. She had to.

Simon lay on his bed, long after Jaz had gone, staring at the lamp, not wanting to turn it out, not wanting to go to sleep.

He'd refused to let anyone in, so after hours of per-suasion and pleading by various workers Dave had eventually used his weight, leaning on the door, forcing the chest of drawers back, allowing Jaz to wriggle in. She'd sat down on the bed beside Simon and picked up one of the articles.

'Leave it!' Simon had snapped, snatching it from her, putting them all back in the envelope with the letter.

'And don't go telling Roz I've got them! 'Cos she's not having 'em back.'

'What's all this about, Simon?' Jaz had asked, looking at all the debris from the drawer, strewn round the floor. 'What's set it all off again?'

'Nothing,' Simon had insisted. 'Nothing's set it off. It's always there. It never goes away. Not for a single flaming minute.'

He hadn't said 'flaming'. He'd said something else. He was sanitising it now, in his head, because he didn't like swearing at Jaz. Wished he hadn't. Wished he hadn't said any of those things to her. But he couldn't help it. Just like he couldn't help the other stuff. It just happened. Like it was someone else doing it. Not him.

He'd lost it completely when she'd suggested a new sort of shrink. A hypno-bloody-therapist or something. Someone who went digging around in your head when you weren't even awake to know what you were saying. As if! As if he was going to let someone do that to him.

'It might help,' Jaz had said, hardly flinching when he called her a stupid bitch. 'Help you to make sense of things. Think about it, eh?'

He didn't need to think about it. He didn't need a hypnotist to summon the ghosts. He knew exactly what it was like. The memories that slunk out like thick, black oil slicks, when you couldn't stop them, when you were defenceless, when you were asleep. Which is why he kept the light on, why he tried to stay awake as long as possible . . .

But you couldn't do it. Especially not when you'd been up all the previous night, prowling around, trying to remember, trying to forget. You just couldn't stop your eyes closing and suddenly you were somewhere else...

A ball whizzing past me straight into the makeshift goal. Wayne Drysdale grabbing the collar of my tee-shirt, yelling in my face so spit goes in my eyes making me blink.

'You're useless you are, Simon! Go on, bugger off home. We're better without you.'

Trying not to cry as I trudge off across the waste ground with the big boys laughing at me, yelling after me. And I know someone else is going to be yelling soon too. My mum 'cos I'm late again. Really late. I look at my watch. The one Auntie Roz bought me for my birthday.

'What's he want a watch for?' Mum had said. 'He's only seven. Probably break it. I mean, he can't even tell the bloody time, can he?'

But I could. Miss Pirelli had taught me. At school. Said I was bright. Jaz says that.

Simon's eyes opened. He got up, paced the room. He didn't want to go back there. Not to the past. Not tonight.

Someone banged on the wall.

'Quit pacing, you bloody lunatic,' Amrit shouted out. 'I'm trying to get some sleep.'

Simon sat in the chair, gripped the arms...

45

As long as you felt yourself gripping, you knew you were awake. But once the grip starts to slacken you drift back and you can't stop yourself...

The sickness, the panic as I look at my watch. I've done it again. Stayed out, hanging round with the big boys. It's quite dark already but Mum won't come looking. She never does. She knows I'm only playing out or at someone's house. She knows I'll turn up sometime. But she'll be mad. Yelling. Swiping me across the head as I try to dart past her up the stairs.

But this night. This night is different. And I don't want to go there. I'm dreaming. I know I'm dreaming. I want to wake up. But I can't. I never can. Not when I've gone this far... I have to go on.

Turning the corner. Seeing the house, seeing the gate. It's open. It's always open. So I run through it, straight up to the door and that's when the door opens too. It opens and he comes out, wiping his hands on his shirt. I see but I don't understand. I don't take it in.

'Don't tell,' he says, dropping to my level, gripping my shoulders, staring at me. 'Don't tell anyone you saw me.'

He says it more than once. But just that. Nothing else. Then he pushes past, knocking me over so I fall on the step, grazing my leg but I still don't get it. Don't know what's going on. So I pick myself up, rush inside, expect my mum to be waiting but she's not. Telly's on, blaring away but she's not watching it. She's not in the kitchen either. At least I don't think so. Not at first. Till I look

46

down. Then I see her. I don't want to. I don't want to look. But I can't stop. My limbs have locked. Holding me there. It's a game. A joke. She's going to get up. She's going to get up. She has to.

'Mum. Please. It's me. Simon. Mum...MUM!'

Simon kept his head down but kept watch, out of the corner of his eye, as Luke strolled over to the breakfast bar, picked up his cereal and sat down next to Amrit, staring all the time at Simon who was sitting on his own.

'Did you hear Si last night?' said Luke in an exaggerated whisper that was loud enough for the whole dining room to hear. 'Shouting for his mummy again! Pathetic.'

Dave bolted from his position by the door, grabbing Simon as he leapt up, overturning the table.

'OK, OK,' said Dave, steering Simon out to the office. 'Let it go. Let it go. I'll deal with Luke. Sit down. I said sit down!'

Simon sat because he was too exhausted to do anything else. He'd been up since the nightmare, since his screams and crashing about, in his haste to get to the loo, had brought care staff running, fussing, talking to him, talking at him. Feeding him tablets to calm him down. Tablets that didn't work. That just made him feel sick.

'I think you'd better stay here today,' Dave was saying. 'Get some rest.'

Simon shook his head.

'No,' he said, though he wasn't sure why. 'I don't want to stay. Not here. I'll go to school. I may as well.'

Dave frowned, as if suspecting Simon's motives.

'Well don't start anything with Luke, eh?'

'It's not me that starts anything! You heard him! You know what he's like.'

'We might have to move one of you, in the end,' said Dave, almost to himself.

'Suits me.'

'I think it would suit all of us,' said Dave. 'But unfortunately it's not that easy. There aren't that many suitable places. It's going to take a while to organise, if it's possible at all. So, for now, you're just going to have to keep out of his way, OK?'

It was definitely OK with Simon. He was happy to keep out of everyone's way, sitting alone in class, finding quiet corners of the school to lurk in at break and lunchtime, managing to avoid everyone until ten minutes before the end of lunch. He'd been sitting on the steps outside the humanities block and had just got up when he saw her coming towards him. Not casually strolling in his direction but coming straight at him, giving him no time to slip away.

He thought he'd solved the problem of Kirsty Broughton but apparently not. He tried a lecherous smile, hoping to intimidate, to remind her of their last encounter but it didn't work. She stood in front of him, shiny blonde hair tied back, uniform impossibly neat. Pretty in a 'little-miss-perfect' sort of way. Not drop dead gorgeous like Jaz but very pretty, even with that scowl on her face and the green eyes narrowed in anger. What was eating her? What had he done this time?

'It was you, wasn't it?' she said.

'Er, we're not back to the park again, are we?' he drawled.

'No we're not back to the park,' said Kirsty, putting down her bag and music case and pulling a newspaper article from her pocket. 'We're in an alleyway this time, with an old woman who's ended up in hospital. So are you going to tell me what the hell you think you're playing at or am I going to the cops?'

Chapter 5

It wasn't quite the way Kirsty had meant it to come out. She'd actually rehearsed the words in her head during her clarinet lesson but, faced with Simon's hostility, it had come out all wrong. She'd aimed for subtle but what she'd got was confrontational.

'I don't know what you're on about,' said Simon, turning away.

'This!' said Kirsty following him, holding the picture in front of his face.

He glanced at it before pushing it away.

'And that's your idea of a joke, is it?' said Kirsty, raising the picture again, forcing him to look properly. 'It was bad enough with me. But her! She's seventy-eight. She stopped to help you! Like I did.'

Kirsty glared at him, waiting for the denial but, as his eyes focused on the picture, he swore, then his expression suddenly changed, the aggression dissolving, giving way to something she didn't recognise.

'I didn't mean it,' said Simon, looking around, refusing to meet her eyes. 'I didn't mean her to fall. I didn't mean her to get hurt. Not like that!'

'So what *did* you mean? Why do it? What the hell—'

She could barely get the words out. It was just so

crazy, so bizarre. Why would anyone do something like that? Why?

'I don't know!' he said, as the questions echoed in her head. 'It just happens. I can't help it.'

'Oh sure,' said Kirsty. 'Can't help covering yourself with fake blood or ketchup or whatever it is you use. Can't help lying down, playing dead.'

'Playing?' said Simon. 'Is that what you think? That it's some sort of game?'

He was shaking now. Not just a slight tremor but visibly shaking like he was going into some sort of fit.

'I'm sorry,' Kirsty found herself saying, as he backed towards the steps, clutched the rail and slumped down.

'I knew she'd fallen,' he was muttering. 'But I didn't know...she'd end up...I didn't mean it!'

Kirsty sat beside him, still holding the newspaper cutting in her hand.

'Put that away,' he said. 'Put it away!'

She scrunched it up, put it in her pocket.

'What am I supposed to think?' she said. 'If it's not a joke.'

He suddenly reached out, gripped her hand really tightly, as if to stop himself shaking.

'Let me see it,' he said. 'The article.'

'You've just told me to put it away,' said Kirsty, trying to free her hand.

'I know. It doesn't matter. Just tell me. What it says. Will they know? Will they know it was me? Could they prove it?'

'I don't think so,' said Kirsty. 'Not from what it says in the paper. Not from what the woman's said so far.'

His grip relaxed and Kirsty pulled her hand away. 'But that's not the point, is it?' she said. 'It's not just about being found out, is it? I mean, I don't think you should wait for that. I don't really know what you're doing or why you're doing it but you ought to tell someone, talk to someone. Get some help.'

'Don't be thick,' said Simon, leaping up. 'I can't, can I? If I tell them what I've done, they'll have me locked up, won't they? In some bloody secure unit.'

'I don't think so ...I don't know,' Kirsty admitted. 'But there must be someone who can help you.'

'I don't want help,' said Simon. 'The last thing I need is more bloody people grubbing about in my life. I can't be doing with it. Not now. Not when I'm—'

'What?' said Kirsty, standing facing him but not too close.

Simon shook his head.

'I can't tell you,' he said. 'There's somethin' I need to do. Summat I need to find out. It's too ...it's sort of complicated. Personal. But please don't go to the cops.'

Kirsty half turned away from him, trying to think, trying to work it out. She ought to do something, now she knew for certain. If not, she'd be an accomplice, wouldn't she? Covering up a crime.

'And what if it happens again?' she said, turning back to him. 'What if you terrify someone else? Hurt someone else?'

'I won't,' said Simon. 'I promise I won't. I'll stop. Honestly.'

'I thought you said you couldn't help it. So how can you stop?'

'I don't know,' said Simon. 'But I will.'

He'd stopped shaking now but he still wouldn't look at her. Not directly.

'And have you done it before?' Kirsty persisted. 'I mean with other people. Not just me and the old lady.'

Simon nodded.

'Not recently,' he muttered. 'But yeah, I've done it before. It's when... when I get... when I...'

He paused as the bell rang.

'I just do crazy things sometimes, all right?' he said, heading towards school.

Kirsty grabbed her bags. Crazy. Paranoid. That's what Briony had said, wasn't it? People thought Simon was a bit paranoid because of something that had happened a long time ago.

'What you're doing,' said Kirsty, hurrying to keep up with him as they approached the main entrance, 'has it got anything to do with... I mean, Briony said...'

'Briony! You've been talking to Briony about me? Oh great! Fantastic! I suppose you know everything now. I suppose the whole bloody school knows.'

'No,' said Kirsty. 'She didn't tell me anything much. Just that something happened... to your mum.'

'Yeah,' said Simon, stopping, moving up close. 'You could say that! My mum was murdered. When I was

53

seven. Stabbed. I was there. I found her. OK? Satisfied
now?'

Jaz was waiting in Simon's room when he got back from
school. He hated the way they did that. Went into your
room when you weren't there, lying in wait like trapdoor
spiders eager for a meal.

'How was school?' Jaz asked.

'Don't bother,' said Simon, slumping into a chair,
'with any of that "how-was-your-day" crap. Just tell me
what you want.'

'Roz has been on the phone,' said Jaz. 'She, er, was
telling me about something that you used to do. When
you were younger.'

'Tearing Ellie's teddies to pieces and burying them in
the garden? Daring Ben to eat the cat's food?' said
Simon. 'I only did that once. He puked up all over the
new rug. And the cats weren't too pleased either.'

'No,' said Jaz. 'Not that. Roz said you used to ... sort
of act out what you'd seen. She'd find you lying on the
kitchen floor, with red paint or ketchup on your chest.
You'd spend ages, acting out the whole thing, Roz said.
Being your mum, being you, being him ...'

'So?' said Simon, standing up, pacing around.
'That's good, isn't it? The psychologist I saw back then
used to give me dolls and a doll's house to play with.
Like I was thick or something. Like I didn't know she
was waiting for me to put Mummy in the kitchen, on
the floor, with the little Simon doll standing over her.

54

Play-acting's supposed to get it out of the system, see?'

'Yeah,' said Jaz. 'I know that! But not when the play-acting hurts someone else. You see the reason Roz told me is that she thinks you might have started doing it again.'

'I haven't.'

'OK,' said Jaz. 'It's just that she read something in the paper.'

'Did she?' said Simon. 'Well, whatever it was, it didn't have nothing to do with me. All that was ages ago. I don't do crazy stuff like that no more.'

Did Jaz believe him? Probably not. Would Roz believe him? Definitely not. It didn't matter anyway. The only one who knew for certain was that Kirsty Broughton. And he'd already decided how to deal with that. As soon as Jaz went, as soon as he got a minute to himself, he was going to sort it out.

Kirsty headed across the park towards the children's play area. Was she crazy? Was she completely out of her mind? Going to meet Simon like this! A lad she barely knew and what she did know of him was hardly reassuring.

The phone call had taken her completely by surprise, not least because he obviously knew her mobile number.

'I got it off one of your friends,' he'd said. 'I just want to talk to you. Explain. You know.'

She'd resisted, at first, but he'd sounded so urgent, desperate almost. The really bizarre thing though, was that she found herself lying to her parents, telling them

the phone call was from Jamie, that she was going round
to Jamie's house. It was half a lie, at any rate. She really
had arranged to see Jamie, later. She could go on there,
after seeing Simon, couldn't she?

It was quite early. Only six o'clock. She'd be away
from the park before it got really dark. There were still
a fair few people around, some young lads playing
football, people walking dogs, even a bloke pushing a
kid on the swings, so she wouldn't be alone with Simon.
There was nothing to worry about.

Simon was sitting on the roundabout, moving it
slowly with his feet, when she arrived. He was wearing
a light grey hoody with a couple of tee shirts underneath,
baggy pants, expensive trainers, looking cool and older
than he did in his school uniform. He stopped the
roundabout and she sat down next to him, her arm
resting on the bar between them. He smiled, looking sort
of shy, like it was a first date or something.

'You said I ought to talk to someone,' he said.

'What?'

'Today, in school, you said I ought to talk to someone.
Tell 'em what I was doing.'

'I meant a teacher!' said Kirsty. 'A professional or
family or something.'

'I can't,' said Simon. 'But I want to tell you. Tell you
why you shouldn't go to the cops.'

'I don't think I was going to,' said Kirsty. 'But...'

'But you think you should? Yeah, I know. Maybe I
think you should too. In a way. But it was an accident. It

56

really was. I never thought...I don't hardly know I'm doing it. Not at the time. Not really. And you were right, I guess. It's all sort of tied up with what happened...to my mum.'

He was talking increasingly rapidly. Spilling out the story so fast, it was hard for Kirsty to keep up. How his parents had split up when he was four. How his dad used to come and see him sometimes. Not often. But he came. How there'd be rows. Mum and Dad shouting at each other. It was all told fairly flatly, without emotion until he came to the night it happened. His voice somehow thickened, tightened. Words rushed out, disjointed, thoughts half-finished as though he was hurling a jigsaw at her piece by piece, expecting her to put it together herself.

'You saw the killer?' Kirsty asked, as Simon finally paused for breath. 'You saw someone come out of the house?'

'Not just someone,' said Simon. 'My dad. It was my dad. He bent down, looked at me but like it wasn't really me at all. As if I was nothing. Just something in his way. He told me not to tell. Not to tell anyone I'd seen him. But I did. I couldn't help it. I told them about the blood on his hands, on his shirt.'

Kirsty found herself shaking her head. It was impossible to believe. Impossible to imagine what it must have been like. Just seven years old. Finding your mum like that, knowing it was your dad who'd killed her. How could anyone ever deal with something like that?

'It was my fault,' said Simon. 'My fault he went to prison. I shouldn't have said anything. But I wanted to tell. I *wanted* him to be locked up. For what he'd done.'

'You did the right thing,' Kirsty began. 'I mean, you couldn't have done anything else, could you?'

'That's what everyone reckons,' said Simon. 'The shrinks. Auntie Roz. Uncle Paul. I went to live with Roz...afterwards...but...'

The words were slow now, as though he was drained, exhausted. Kirsty noticed that the man and his kid had left the swings. The only person she could see was a youngish woman striding across the grass with a spaniel bounding in front of her. Kirsty shivered and rubbed her hands together. She was wearing jeans, jumper, jacket but it was cold sitting so still, though Simon didn't seem to notice at all.

'It was a mess,' he was saying. '*I* was a mess. Completely hyper. Couldn't do anything, couldn't concentrate on anything. Nightmares every night.'

He stopped, looked at Kirsty, as if expecting her to say something. But what *could* she say? What could she possibly say that wouldn't sound trite, inadequate?

'I'm not asking for sympathy,' he said, misinterpreting the silence. 'I know it's not an excuse. For the stuff I do. I've been told often enough. I mean, I was getting better, well a bit, I think. After all the years of therapy and stuff but then I found the letter, didn't I?'

A sudden burst of noise startled Kirsty, startled both of them. She reached into her pocket, pulled out her mobile, half-glad of the interruption until she noticed the number.

'Hi, Mum,' she said.

'Kirsty, where are you?'

'Er, with Jamie.'

'No you're not. Jamie's here! He called round for you.'

Kirsty glanced at her watch. She wasn't supposed to be meeting Jamie for another half-hour. Trust him to change the arrangements, to be early for once, to screw up!

'I think you'd better come home, don't you?' her mother said.

'Trouble?' said Simon, as Kirsty put the phone away.

'Sort of,' said Kirsty. 'I have to go. But—'

'I'll walk back with you,' said Simon, standing up.

She expected him to carry on where they'd left off, to talk about the letter but he didn't.

'Roz and Paul were really good to me, I suppose,' he said, staring straight ahead as if he was talking to himself, rather than to her. 'Paul especially, at first. Took me to counselling and stuff but I reckon they thought it would be like magic, or summat. Get it all sorted in a couple of months. Then, when it didn't, they got fed up, I guess. Started accusing me of not trying. Like I didn't want to get over it. But, in a way, they were making it worse, see?'

He turned to look at her, as they approached the park gate.

'Say something!' he said. 'Or I'll be ramblin' on all

night! I didn't mean to tell you all this stuff. I haven't even got to the point yet.'

He'd told her to say something but he didn't give her a chance.

'The thing is,' he said, as they walked out onto the road. 'At first, it was all about my mum. But then it started to be more about my dad and that's what Roz and Paul made worse. 'Cos they were always like going on about him. What a shit he was. How Mum should never have got together with him in the first place. How he didn't even care about me at all. Pushing me away, running off, leaving me to find her, like that.'

Kirsty stopped walking. They'd reached the corner of her street.

'You want me to turn back now, right?' Simon asked.

'Yeah,' said Kirsty. 'It might be best. Jamie's at our house and he's already a bit paranoid about you! And I think it's best if I tell Mum I was with Sonja or something...but finish what you were going to tell me.'

'Yeah well,' said Simon. 'I suppose I sort of believed them, about my dad, but then I found this letter and ...ah,' he added, glancing up the street. 'I think it might have to wait. Your boyfriend's come looking for you.'

Kirsty turned to see Jamie walking towards them and, when she turned back, Simon was already striding away.

'What were you doing with him?' Jamie asked, as they met up.

'I just bumped into him, on my way round to yours,' Kirsty said.

'Oh yeah,' said Jamie, following her towards the house. 'As if!'

Jamie slammed the gate and, at the same time, the front door opened and Kirsty's mum appeared.

'Kirsty, where on earth have you been?' she said. 'I was worried sick when Jamie turned up and said he hadn't seen you!'

'Oh for goodness' sake,' said Kirsty, pushing past. 'What's wrong with you people? I bumped into a friend, that's all!'

'Yeah well I wouldn't get too friendly with him,' Jamie muttered.

'Who?' asked Kirsty's mum.

'Simon Wells,' said Jamie. 'New lad at school. The one whose dad's in gaol for murdering his mum.'

'How do you know that?' said Kirsty.

'Luke Harris told me,' said Jamie. 'When he was showing me the two stitches he had to have over his eye after Simon had a go at him for no reason. Luke reckons the temper thing must run in the family, see?'

'Does he?' Kirsty snapped.

'Well, I'm sure it's not genetic or anything,' said Mum. 'But I think Jamie's right, love. It might be best not to get too friendly.'

'Thanks, Jamie,' Kirsty hissed, as her mum wandered off. 'I'm never going to hear the last of this now. You know what Mum's like.'

Jamie shrugged.

'Are we going out or what?' he said. 'Tony's invited

everyone round his tonight.'

'You go,' said Kirsty. 'I don't feel like it.'

'Oh come on,' said Jamie. 'Sonja's going and Carlo and ... Laura.'

'Well that'll be nice,' said Kirsty, storming upstairs. 'Enjoy it.'

Chapter 6

'Oh good,' said Dave, accosting Simon as soon as he got back to Oakfields. 'You've remembered.'

Simon stared around, looking for clues. Remembered? What was he supposed to have remembered? What was Dave on about?

'He's just arrived,' Dave added, pointing to the office.

Simon looked through the glass door and saw the guy with the bushy, grey beard. Colin, his social worker. One of the army of professionals who were supposed to help him. This was obviously a pre-booked appointment, a routine visit, nothing to worry about and, with any luck, it would be over fairly quickly. Simon's phone beeped as he went in and sat down opposite Colin. He glanced at the text message, a single word, 'stop'.

What the hell was that about? Some sort of bizarre advert, probably. He deleted it, shoved his phone back in his pocket and smiled at Colin. Best to be co-operative, to play the game. Besides, Colin was all right. It was Colin who'd taken him to see his dad. Twice now they'd been and Colin was supposed to be fixing up another visit soon. The trouble with social workers though, was that they couldn't just do things, they had to talk about them too. Colin was off almost straight away, asking him how he'd felt since the last visit, what he'd been doing, what he'd been thinking about.

'I've been fine,' Simon muttered. 'Haven't really thought about it.'

It was impossible to tell him. Tell him how many times he'd heard the clunk of those prison gates, how many nightmares he'd had, how he'd started acting freaky again. Did Colin know? Had he read the newspaper? Had he guessed? Had he discussed it with Roz and Paul or with Jaz?

Simon could tell Colin was disappointed with his responses but he couldn't give him anything else, which was weird, in a way, because he'd given Kirsty far too much. Somehow, with her, it had all come spilling out, far too much background, far too much detail, far more than he'd ever intended to say. Why? He hardly knew her. At first, she'd taken him by surprise, showing him the picture of the old woman like that, so his expression had given him away and all the wrong words had gushed out, confession instead of denial.

Then, he'd deliberately tried to play on her sympathy to stop her going to the cops but there was more to it than that. There was something about her, her directness, which made her easy to talk to. She didn't have any hidden agendas like the professionals, and, unlike Briony, Simon didn't think she'd blab. She was smart too, the sort of person who'd know things, be able to work stuff out and he needed someone like that right now.

'So it'll be two weeks tomorrow,' Colin was saying.

'Sorry?'

'The next visit to your dad,' Colin said. 'You'll have to have a day off school but I guess that won't bother you too much.'

Two weeks, Simon thought, as Colin left. That's why he needed Kirsty's help. Because he wanted to make a bit more progress before he saw his dad again and two weeks didn't give him much time.

'I didn't go to Tony's last night,' Jamie told Kirsty in registration on Wednesday. 'I went straight home. Didn't think it'd be any good without you. Kirsty, are you listening?'

Kirsty wasn't. Not really. She was thinking about the envelope in her pocket, the one Simon had shoved into her hand as they'd walked into the classroom. Did he want to meet up again? Finish what he'd been telling her? But why write her a note? Why not send a text or just ask her outright? Notes didn't seem Simon's style somehow. Anyway, whatever it contained, it was impossible to read it in tutor time or in English, while she was sitting next to Jamie. In period 2, she was with Sonja but still didn't fancy getting the note out, not least because it was Mr Felton, who was obviously psychic because of the way he knew, instinctively, when someone wasn't working.

So she waited till break, settled herself in a quiet corner of the library and took out the envelope. It was just plain brown with nothing written on the front but, as she pulled out the piece of paper, she realised it wasn't a note, as such, at all. It was a letter, a handwritten letter, on prison notepaper. The letter Simon had been talking about last night?

Kirsty checked that no one was heading her way, leant over the desk, her arm shielding the letter and started to read.

Dear Simon,

I know you won't answer this, you probably won't even read it. Roz says you don't want to know me and I can't blame you. But I keep writing in the hope that as you get older you'll change your mind because I need you to know that I'm so sorry for what I did.

Kirsty looked up. Sorry seemed a bit inadequate somehow but, glancing back to the letter, she realised she'd misunderstood. He wasn't apologising for the murder.

I should never have run off and left you like that. I still can't believe I did that. No matter how shocked I was, how scared, I shouldn't have done it. I should have thought of you, Simon, not myself. I didn't then but I do now, all the time. I wonder what you're like now and how you're getting on. And I wonder whether I'll ever see you, ever get a chance to explain. I don't much care about what anyone else thinks but I care about you.

Why? Why had Simon given her this? It was so personal, like prying into someone's diary, wrong but compulsive. Kirsty turned over. The letter went on in the same way for a while, sort of rambling, repetitive, disjointed, then it settled down, drifting on to life in prison, the routine, other inmates, some courses Simon's dad had done, the qualifications he'd got.

Shouldn't think they'll do me too much good, he wrote, because I don't think they'll be letting me out anytime soon.

It was weird, Kirsty thought, just how many emotions the letter was stirring up, even though she didn't know the guy, so she could barely imagine how it must have affected Simon, finding something like this. Hearing footsteps behind her, she slid the letter under her bag, just as someone sat down.

'It's OK, it's me,' Simon whispered, pulling a chair out and sitting beside her.

She retrieved the letter and passed it to him.

'I thought it'd be easier,' he said, answering her unspoken question. 'If I just let you read it, rather than trying to tell you.'

'Why though?' said Kirsty. 'Why tell me at all?'

'I dunno,' said Simon, edging his chair a little closer. 'I just thought you could help.'

Kirsty leant back a bit, wishing that Simon were just a touch less attractive, that he didn't have such an effect on her. It was like with Jamie, only more intense. What was it with her and the wrong sort of boys? Why couldn't she pick nice steady types, like Sonja's boyfriend, Carlo? Even as a friend, Simon could be trouble, was already trouble.

'What sort of help?' she asked.

'I dunno,' said Simon again. 'I just need someone to talk to, someone to help me sort it out. The thing is, Dad always reckoned he was innocent.'

'Innocent?' said Kirsty.

'Yeah,' said Simon. 'I mean, I always knew that's what he'd said. That's why he's still inside, see? If he'd pleaded guilty, said it was a spur of the moment thing, a row that went wrong, he might only have been charged with manslaughter. Or if he'd admit to it, even now, show remorse and all that, he could get the sentence reduced. But he won't. He insists he didn't do it.'

'But you said you saw him!' said Kirsty.

'I saw him coming *out*,' said Simon. 'And 'cos of that and with all the sort of circumstantial evidence, they never even looked for anyone else.'

'Well, obviously I don't know all the details,' said Kirsty. 'But I mean it sounds —'

'Yeah, exactly,' said Simon. 'The police were convinced. The jury was convinced. Roz and Paul were convinced. And I was too. I mean, it just seemed sort of obvious. But then I found the letter and it set off a massive row with Roz and Paul, 'cos they'd been lying, they'd never told me he'd been in touch or anything.'

'They maybe thought they were doing it for the best,' said Kirsty. 'Trying to protect you or something.'

'Yeah, I know that,' said Simon. 'And maybe that was

OK at first, when I was little but not now. I'm old enough to make up my own mind. So, I went to see him in prison. And all the stuff Roz always said about him, it don't seem right somehow.'

'Like what?'

'Like him being a loser, a waster, a boozer, a womaniser. I mean, I know he wasn't no saint. I remember him being pissed a lot and he was never exactly around for me, if you know what I mean. But, when I saw him, when I talked to him—'

'People change,' said Kirsty, gently. 'Especially in prison, I guess. He's had time to think about things.'

'Yeah,' said Simon. 'And I started to think too. What if everyone was wrong about him? Even if he was all those things, it doesn't make him a murderer, does it? So what if he really didn't do it? He's been inside, for ten years, because of me, because of what I said.'

'They wouldn't have convicted him just on your evidence,' said Kirsty. 'They don't do that. There must have been something else.'

'They found his prints all over the place,' said Simon. 'Even on the knife. And don't say it! I know. That's a bit sort of damning, yeah? But he could have picked the knife up. Off the floor. Like he said. Without thinking.'

'Is this what you were talking about?' said Kirsty. 'Is this what you want to do? Find out if he's really guilty or not? But, Simon, it's crazy—'

'Thanks,' said Simon, standing up. 'But I don't need

you to tell me I'm crazy. I've got plenty of people doing that.'

'I didn't mean *you* were crazy,' said Kirsty, following him, as the bell started to ring, almost drowning out her words. 'I mean *it's* crazy. How can you possibly find out after all these years? How would you even start?'

'I already have,' said Simon, veering off to the left and walking into a classroom.

As soon as the bell went for lunch, Kirsty darted out of science intending to look for Simon. She'd barely gone three paces down the corridor when she started to pick up on a conversation from a group of rowdy lads spilling out of one of the other science labs.

'That were brill, that was! Dead funny.'

'Yeah but what did Luke say to set him off?'

'Dunno but Simon was in a right mood already. The look on Mrs Crow's face when Si walked out. It were classic!'

'Er, is this Simon Wells you're talking about?' said Kirsty, stopping one of the lads.

'Yeah.'

'So where's he gone?' said Kirsty, urgently. 'Simon? Where's he gone? Is he still in school?'

'I dunno, do I?' said the lad.

Kirsty hurried along the corridor, down the stairs and out into the playground. She looked round, wondering where to start. The school wasn't that big but there were plenty of places for Simon to lurk if he really didn't want to be found. She knew, from past experience, that it could take ages to find him and besides, the chances were he wasn't in school anyway. So why not just leave it? Let him get on with whatever it was he thought he was doing. But she couldn't. It was partly her fault that he'd got in a mood and, as Luke had made it worse, there was no telling what Simon might do. What if he pulled his crazy stunt again? Playing dead. She couldn't let him do that. She had at least to try to track him down.

She leant against the wall and took out her mobile, watching all the time for prowling teachers. You weren't supposed to use mobiles in school or even have them switched on. Hers hadn't been but she guessed Simon wouldn't take too much notice of rules like that and that his would be. She'd stored his number, but even if it rang out, he probably wouldn't answer. Maybe a text message would be better. She tried the call first and was surprised when he answered straight away.

'Where are you?' she asked.

'Bus station,' he said.

'The bus station?' she repeated.

What was he doing there? How had he got into town so quickly?

'Well, get yourself back,' she said, cursing herself for sounding just like her mum or a teacher or something. 'Running away isn't going to help, is it? You need to get things sorted out.'

'I can't,' he said. 'Not now. Not yet. I'd kill him if he starts on me again.'

71

Kirsty shivered. He didn't mean it. Not literally. Everyone said stuff like that when they were angry. Simon didn't really mean he'd kill Luke.

'So what are you doing?' she said. 'Where are you planning on going?'

'Come with me,' he said. 'And find out.'

'Come with you?' said Kirsty, as her phone started to crackle. 'Now?'

He didn't answer. Maybe he thought it was a stupid question.

'All right,' said Kirsty, glancing at the time. 'Stay there. Wait for me.'

It wasn't too difficult to slip out of the school gates. There were a few pupils going home for lunch and dozens of sixth formers heading into town, so it was only a matter of blending with the crowd but Kirsty was still nervous. She'd never played truant before. Not ever. She wasn't doing it now, she told herself, fastening up her jacket. It would only take fifteen minutes or so to get to the bus station and, of course, she had no intention of going anywhere with Simon. She was just going to talk to him so she'd easily be back in time for afternoon lessons, hopefully taking Simon with her.

He was waiting by the entrance and smiled as she approached but his eyes looked strained, anxious, pained almost, as they always did. The minute she reached him, he began to move away, towards one of the stops.

'Bus'll be here in a couple of minutes,' he said.

'Which bus?' Kirsty asked. 'Where are you going?'

'Home.'

'You don't need to catch a bus to Oakfields.'

'That's not home, is it?'

'But if you go back to your auntie's—'

'I'm not going there neither. I'm going home.'

'Home as in—'

'Yeah,' said Simon. 'Where I used to live. With my mum.'

'But why?' said Kirsty. 'What good will that do?'

'There's a guy I need to see,' he said as a bus turned the corner and headed their way. 'May as well do it now 'cos I'm not going back to school. Not today.'

'Why not?' said Kirsty. 'The longer you leave it, the worse it'll get.'

'No,' said Simon. 'I've got to stay away from Luke. He does my head in. Just winds me up. All the bloody time. Going on and on about what happened to my mum.'

'Why?' said Kirsty. 'Why does he do that?'

'Dunno,' said Simon. 'He's a nutter. Winds everyone up. But he seems to specially have it in for me. Probably gets more reaction out of me than he does out of some of the others. I nearly hit him again, in science. But I didn't. So that's good, innit? Jaz says I should walk away from trouble and I have, haven't I?'

'I don't think she meant you should walk out of school!'

'Too late,' said Simon. 'I already have. Now are you coming with me or what?'

73

'I can't,' said Kirsty. 'Mr Lane's bound to notice if I'm not in registration.'

'He won't bother,' said Simon. 'They'll all be too busy running round looking for me. I mean, they won't think *you're* bunking off, will they?'

He grabbed her hand, virtually pulling her onto the bus.

'If you're worried about it,' he said, as the bus pulled away, 'phone one of your mates. Tell 'em to cover for you.'

Kirsty phoned Sonja.

'I've got a dentist appointment,' Kirsty lied. 'Mum's just phoned to remind me. So tell Mr Lane, will you?'

As she ended the call, Kirsty noticed that her credit was nearly out. Barely enough left for an emergency call. If she needed to make one. If she got stuck anywhere. If there was a problem.

'Er, this bloke you need to see,' Kirsty began.

'The thing is,' said Simon, 'when I found the letter, I found other stuff as well. Solicitor's letters. All the old newspaper reports.'

Kirsty wondered what exactly Simon meant by 'found'. It seemed unlikely that his aunt and uncle would have left stuff like that lying around. So had Simon deliberately gone looking?

'Anyway,' said Simon. 'It got me thinking and then when I went to see my dad, it brought a whole load of memories back. Just like Roz and Paul said it would, I suppose. Too many in some ways but not enough in others, if you know what I mean.'

Kirsty didn't, not really and, important as it was, she was finding it difficult to concentrate. She hadn't eaten and the bumpy motion of the bus was making her feel sick. Or maybe it was the panic. The fact that she didn't really know where she was going or what she was doing here. What if Mr Lane checked up on her? What if her parents found out she was bunking off? They'd go ballistic.

'You OK?' said Simon, looking genuinely concerned. 'You've gone a bit sort of green.'

'I'm all right. Go on.'

'Well, I know Roz says Dad's a liar and all that. But even if he is, that don't mean he's lying about this, does it? There's a whole load of stuff that doesn't make sense.'

'Like what?'

'I know this is gonna sound crazy,' said Simon. 'But like the way I feel, for a start. I mean, after it happened, I hated him, right? Or thought I did. But when I saw him...it was like...like I was a kid again. Looking at my dad. Getting that feeling you get when you're little. When you think your parents are perfect. No matter what they do.'

Kirsty nodded, trying to understand.

'Well, I couldn't feel like that, could I?' said Simon. 'I couldn't still love him like that if...you can't love someone who killed your mum, can you?'

Kirsty shook her head, all attempts at understanding evaporating. She didn't know. Had no way of even imagining.

'And he's like totally obsessed with proving his innocence,' said Simon. 'It's all he thinks about, all he talks about. He's had two appeals already. They've both failed but he's still at it. He wouldn't do that, would he? If he knew, deep down, he was guilty. He'd have given up long ago.'

Kirsty was about to speak but Simon didn't give her a chance.

'There's other stuff too,' he went on. 'That might just help with the next appeal. I'll show you. When we get back. It might not mean anything but if it does, if Dad's telling the truth, if he didn't kill Mum, then someone else did, yeah?'

The sickness in Kirsty's stomach suddenly gushed up to her throat. She pulled a tissue from her pocket, held it to her mouth, leant back in her seat and tried to breathe deeply. What did Simon mean? What did he think he was doing? What was he dragging her into?

'Hey,' Simon said. 'What is it? What's wrong?'

'Er, this bloke we're going to see,' said Kirsty, when she was sure the nausea had subsided. 'This isn't some vigilante mission, is it? You don't think he's the real killer or anything, do you?'

Chapter 7

'What sort of loony do you take me for?' said Simon. 'Even if he was, I wouldn't just march up to him and accuse him, would I? Or try some stupid revenge stunt. I only want to talk to him.'

'And that's all?' said Kirsty. 'Just talk.'

'Yeah,' said Simon. 'I'm not playing detective, trying to track down the murderer myself or anything. But if I could just find *something*. Something that'll help Dad. And I think I might have done, see? So I just need to check summat. According to the reports and everything, this neighbour was the last person to see Mum before—'

'So you've arranged to see him?' said Kirsty. 'You know he still lives round there?'

'No and no,' said Simon. 'But I reckon he might still be around. It's not the sort of area people move out of much. There's nowhere else for 'em to go.'

Kirsty glanced out of the window, as the bus turned a corner. With listening to Simon and feeling ill, she hadn't taken much notice of where they were going and didn't recognise where they were. The bus had just left a fairly major road and was now meandering round the edges of an estate full of small nineteen fifties houses, some well cared for with neatly

77

trimmed hedges, others a bit shabby with gardens full of junk. There were a couple of derelict shops with windows boarded up.

'Nearly there,' said Simon. 'At least I think so. It's funny. I don't remember it like I thought I would. Maybe it's all changed.'

This was utterly crazy, Kirsty thought. She shouldn't be here. She should be back in school, having a laugh with Sonja, doing normal things, not getting tied up in something she couldn't even begin to understand.

'Er, this might be it, I think,' said Simon. 'We get off here.'

'Simon,' she said, as they got off the bus. 'This thing about your dad being innocent. I know you want to believe it but I keep thinking about him running away. Why would he do that if he had nothing to hide?'

'He panicked,' said Simon. 'He'd already got convictions, see? For nicking cars, getting into fights and stuff. And you know what the cops are like. He knew they'd never believe him. And he was right, wasn't he? They didn't. They didn't believe him about the phone call or anything.'

'What phone call?'

'Hang on,' said Simon. 'I think we go down here. Then it's the next on the left.'

'What was the phone call?' Kirsty prompted.

'Dad reckons Mum phoned him, earlier that night. And that much was definitely true 'cos the cops checked. Anyway, according to Dad, Mum asked him to come round. She sounded paranoid, uptight. Said she had something to tell him.'

'And what about you?' said Kirsty. 'Do you remember her being uptight or anything?'

'Not that day. Not especially. She was always sort of...up and down. I don't know. I was seven! The memories aren't clear like that.'

'It's OK,' said Kirsty, seeing Simon's shoulders tense.

'I remember this road,' said Simon. 'I remember running along here, that night. It's what I see, all the time, in my dream. And as soon as you turn the corner, you can see the house. I remember seeing the gate was open.'

He paused as they turned the corner into a cul-de-sac. He looked down the street, then at Kirsty.

'I was wrong,' he said. 'You can't see it from here. The road curves, the house is set back. I couldn't have seen the house from here or the gate swinging open. It's the dream I'm remembering.'

He shook his head looking confused, distraught.

'The dream must be wrong,' he said. 'That's what I mean. About the memories. They're all screwed up, aren't they? How can you know what's right, what's real?'

He didn't wait for an answer, not that Kirsty could have given one. Simon hurried on and Kirsty followed, looking round at the houses, the parked cars and vans, a grey cat sitting on a window ledge. From inside one of the houses, Kirsty could hear loud music but, apart from that and the cat, there were no other signs of life. Simon stopped outside a house about halfway down. A house that was very much like all the others except that it had new PVC window frames, a wrought-iron gate and low matching railings.

'Ours was wooden,' said Simon, touching the fence. 'This is new. I wonder if they know? The people who live here now. I wonder if they know what happened here? They must do, mustn't they? I wonder if it bothers them? If they think about it? It's weird. I mean, I don't feel anything. I thought I'd be . . . but I'm not. I don't feel upset or nothing.'

He was talking quickly, breathlessly. His face, his hands, even his eyes, were draining of colour, belying his words. He suddenly swung round, stared across the street, then turned back.

'I can't remember whether he lived opposite or next door.'

'Do you remember him at all?' said Kirsty. 'Or is it just from what you've read, what your dad told you?'

'Mixture,' Simon said. 'I sort of remember. Mum called him Mac but that's not his real name. He was always round our place. Doing bits of jobs. Gingerish hair. Tall. Thin. It was next door I think,' he added, wandering to the left. 'Yeah, this one, maybe.'

The house Simon was looking at was a bit run down. No gate, no fence, no hedge of any sort, so Simon walked up the path and rang the bell. There was no sound from the bell, no movement from inside.

'Try knocking,' Kirsty said. 'Bell's obviously knackered.'

At first there was no response to the knock either but then they heard someone shuffling towards the door.

'Yes?' an elderly, female voice shouted.

'Er, does Mac live here?' Simon shouted back.

'Number 34, two doors down,' said the voice.

'Thanks,' said Kirsty, following Simon who was already heading towards Mac's house.

This house had a doorbell that worked and the door opened almost immediately but the guy who stood there couldn't possibly be Mac, Kirsty thought. He was only about her height, smaller than Simon, but quite thick set with a noticeable paunch. So he wasn't tall or thin but the receding brown hair had a gingery tint so maybe... Simon had only been seven. Any adult would have seemed tall then and it was easy enough to put weight on over ten years.

'Mac?' Simon was saying.

'Yeah,' said the man. 'Who wants to know?'

'I'm Simon. Simon Wells.'

Mac peered at Simon and murmured a string of words, most of them rude.

'So who's this?' he said.

'Er, Kirsty,' said Simon. 'Kirsty Broughton,' he added, as Mac continued to stare. 'She's a friend.'

Kirsty shuddered, somehow wishing Simon hadn't given her full name.

'Is she?' said Mac. 'And what do you and your friend want?'

81

'I just wanted to talk to you,' said Simon. 'About what happened. You know.'

' 'Course I bloody know,' said Mac. 'And I did all the talking ten years ago. I'm not gonna do it again. Not for anyone.'

'Simon's not just anyone,' Kirsty found herself saying. 'It was his mum. You can't blame him for wanting to know.'

'He probably wouldn't like it if I told him,' said Mac.

'It doesn't matter whether I like it or not,' said Simon. 'As long as I get it straightened out. In my head. You went round there that night, yeah?'

'Yeah,' said Mac. 'The bath tap was leaking. Pouring water. Washer had gone, so I changed it. That brother-in-law of hers was supposed to do it but he hadn't turned up so she asked me. She was always asking me to do stuff, getting me round there and the wife didn't like it.'

He glanced over his shoulder, as if 'the wife' might be listening from somewhere in the house.

'She was hard to resist, your mum,' Mac added. 'Had a bit of a way with men, if you know what I mean.'

'Never mind that,' Simon snapped. 'What happened after you'd fixed the tap?'

'I came home,' said Mac. 'Then later on I heard shouting. Your mum and dad yellin' at each other.'

'You sure it was Dad?'

'Sounded like him.'

'But you're not sure?'

'Not hundred per cent but I reckon it must have been.'

'And what time was it?' said Simon.

'Maybe eightish, half past. I don't know!' said Mac. 'It was ten years ago. I told the cops at the time but I can't remember now!'

'And did your wife hear the shouts?' said Simon, trying to look past Mac into the house.

'No, she was out, round her mother's,' he said, as if repeating something he'd learnt off by heart.

'And you didn't do nothing?' said Simon. 'You didn't go and see what the shouting was about?'

'God, you're worse than the bloody cops, you are,' said Mac. 'No I didn't go round 'cos it wasn't what you'd call unusual. There was always something going on. If it wasn't your dad it'd be—'

'Who?' said Simon. 'Who else could it have been?'

'Look,' said Mac, dropping his voice. 'You were only a kid at the time. You maybe didn't realise, don't remember and maybe it's best left that way.'

'Tell me,' said Simon.

Mac looked at Simon, then at Kirsty, biting his top lip, putting his hand up to his chin, as if deciding what to say, how to say it.

'If it wasn't your dad round there kicking off,' said Mac, 'it'd be some other bloke. Different ones. All the bloody time. During the day when you were at school, at night when you were in bed. The wife even phoned the social services a couple of times. Said it were disgusting, bringing a kid up like that but—'

'What are you trying to say?' said Simon.

83

'I don't know how I can make it any clearer,' said Mac, looking at Kirsty, as if afraid to offend her, as if she was the one who mattered. 'There were always men around. Paying for services, OK?'

'A prozzie?' said Simon, his face burning. 'Is that what you're saying? That my mum was on the game? No. No way. You're lying. It isn't true.'

'Sorry,' said Mac. 'Don't shoot the messenger. You said you wanted to know and I've told you.'

'I said I wanted the truth,' yelled Simon. 'Not a pack of bloody lies.'

He lurched forward but Mac pushed him back.

'Don't mess with me, sonny,' said Mac. 'Or you'll be sorry. And I wouldn't go snooping much further, if I were you. 'Cos your mum was mixed up with a couple of very nasty people. People who wouldn't thank you for dredging it all up again, right?'

'What people?' said Simon. 'Did you tell the cops all this, at the time?'

'Sort of,' said Mac. 'Without naming names. Didn't have to. The cops weren't interested. It was nothing to do with all that, was it?'

'All what?' said Simon.

'Didn't Lou tell you?' Mac asked. 'When you went to see her the other week?'

'How do you know about that?' said Simon.

'Word gets round,' said Mac. 'And to a lot of the wrong people, if you know what I mean.'

'No, I don't,' said Simon.

Kirsty certainly didn't. Who was Lou? Why hadn't Simon mentioned her? Who were these people Mac kept going on about?

'I really am gonna have to spell it out for you, aren't I?' said Mac. 'The drug guys. Your mum was on the game to pay for her drugs, OK? And I don't just mean a bit of dope either. Maybe that's what the last row with your dad was about. Her drugs and her men. I don't know, do I?'

'No,' said Simon. 'It couldn't have been. 'Cos it's not true. None of it's true.'

'Look, sonny,' said Mac. 'You asked and I told you. If you don't believe it, fine. It's up to you. Now piss off and leave me alone.'

Mac stepped back inside and slammed the door. Simon leant forward, pressed the bell, and carried on pressing it, until Kirsty grabbed his arm.

'Come on,' she said. 'It won't do any good.'

'It's not true,' said Simon, as they walked away from the house. 'It's not true. She didn't do any of that stuff. She couldn't have done.'

The words were definite enough but there was something in Simon's tone that sounded uncertain.

'So who's this Lou you went to see?' Kirsty asked.

'Louise,' said Simon. 'My gran. Sort of.'

'What do you mean, sort of?'

'My family's a bit complicated,' said Simon. 'My mum's mum walked out when Mum and Roz were little. Just took off and they never heard from her again. Then

85

their dad, my granddad, shacked up with this Louise. You following so far?'

Kirsty nodded.

'Good,' said Simon. ''Cos that's the easy bit. Then when Roz and Mum were about eight and ten, their dad left Lou and went off with someone else, see? The girls went with him but this other woman already had three kids and was expecting another, so it was kind of messy. Mum started bunking off school, getting into bother; so after six months or so Roz packed their bags and decided they were both gonna go back to Lou.'

'But Lou wasn't a real relation?' said Kirsty. 'A blood relation.'

'No, but she took them in, anyway,' said Simon. 'She's all right, is Lou. In a way. So it was OK for a year or so until this guy called Ian moved in with Lou. Mum and Roz didn't like him and there was some sort of bother with his sons.'

'What sort of bother?'

'Mum accused them of . . . trying to do stuff to her . . . you know.'

'Blimey,' said Kirsty, shuddering. 'She'd only be about eleven or twelve, wouldn't she? I mean, how old were they?'

'Nineteen, I think,' said Simon. 'At the time. They were twins. Anyway, Ian stood up for 'em. Said Mum was just trying to cause trouble. Lou sided with Ian and the lads. Their dad didn't want 'em back so Mum and Roz ended up in care. Roz settled in a foster home eventually but Mum kept running off, living rough and stuff.'

Kirsty shook her head, trying to imagine someone younger than she was now, not wanted by any of their family, living out on the streets.

'Told you it were complicated,' said Simon. 'Anyway Mum used to drift back and see Lou sometimes, though Roz wouldn't have nothing to do with her. Still won't. Never really forgave Lou for dumping her in care, which is funny really 'cos that's exactly what Roz has done to me, innit? Anyway, Roz doesn't like anything to do with the past and stuff but I thought Lou might know something so I went to see her.'

'And did she?' Kirsty asked.

'Well, most of what I've just told you,' said Simon. 'But nothing much about the later stuff. After Mum went into care, after she met my dad and everything. I think Lou feels a bit guilty, like Roz. I mean, that's the trouble. No one wants to talk about it. Roz never told me anything.'

'I can understand why Lou might feel a bit responsible,' said Kirsty. 'But why would Roz have anything to hide?'

Simon didn't have a chance to answer, as Kirsty's phone rang. She glanced at the number, glanced at her watch.

'Oh great!' she said. 'Just great.'

Chapter 8

'I've said I'm sorry!' Jamie muttered as he followed Kirsty towards the Head of Year's office.

'Is that sorry you happened to tell Sonja I didn't have a dental appointment?' said Kirsty. 'Or sorry you just happened to say it loud enough for Mr Lane to hear? Or maybe you mean sorry for mentioning that I might have gone off with Simon!'

'I didn't mean to get you into bother.'

'Oh, don't worry,' said Kirsty, sweetly. 'You didn't. The school phoned my dad. Dad phoned me. My parents got in a flap and left work early. Mum went round to Oakfields, while Dad gave me a ten-hour lecture until Mum came home and then it started all over again. Oh yes, and now I've got to see Killer Kershaw about bunking off, so no bother, Jamie, no bother at all.'

She joined a queue of three other miscreants outside Mrs Kershaw's office.

'I don't know why you had to go running after Simon in the first place,' Jamie mumbled.

'No?' said Kirsty. 'Well, as it's none of your bloody business, it doesn't really matter, does it? Oh, and you needn't bother with any more heavy breathing.'

'Uh?' said Jamie.

'Don't play the innocent, Jamie. You know what I mean. Your stupid phone calls!'

'What phone calls? What are you on about?'

'Last night,' said Kirsty. 'Phone kept ringing and every time Dad picked up, it went dead.'

'It's them call centre things,' said Jamie. 'They do that, don't they? Phone a whole load of people and put most of them on hold.'

'We've had cold calls blocked,' said Kirsty. 'And besides, when *I* answered it was different, wasn't it?'

She stared at Jamie, waiting for a reaction but the bemusement on his face never faltered.

'You got a perv?' he said. 'A heavy breather?'

'At first,' said Kirsty. 'Then a warning.'

'A warning? What sort of warning?'

'You don't know?' Kirsty asked.

'Of course I don't bloody know.'

'Someone warning me to keep away from Simon,' said Kirsty, shuddering at the memory of the voice, thick, disguised, distorted.

'Did you do a 1471?'

'No,' said Kirsty. 'I sort of guessed the number would be withheld and besides, I was sure it was you, mucking about. It was you, wasn't it?'

Jamie shook his head, looked genuinely concerned.

'No,' he said. 'I wouldn't do nothing like that. Can't think who would. I mean, I know loads of people who'd tell you to keep away from Simon 'cos he's a nutter. But they'd tell you to your face, like I do. They wouldn't make sleazy calls.'

Jamie was about to speak again when the door opened and Mrs Kershaw appeared, holding a piece of paper.

'Next,' she said, glancing at the paper. 'Jamie, did I ask to see you?'

'Er, no, Miss.'

'Well get to assembly.'

Mrs Kershaw looked at her list again as Jamie scurried off.

'Simon Wells?' she said. 'Has anyone seen him?'

'I don't think he's in yet, Miss,' Kirsty said.

Mrs Kershaw tutted, ushered Sanjay inside and slammed the door. She clearly wasn't in one of her better moods, though Sanjay hadn't looked too worried. Neither did Lee and Tracy who were next in line but then they were regulars here, used to trouble, like Simon. Simon, who was an even bigger pain than Jamie!

'Don't tell 'em where we've been, what we've been doing,' Simon had said after she'd taken the call on her mobile from her dad. 'I 'aven't told no one about seeing Lou and stuff. It'll only set Roz and Paul off again. So just say we were in town or something.'

Unfortunately Simon hadn't followed his own instructions. Apparently, halfway through the questioning he'd lost his temper, flipped out, started mouthing off, informing Roz and anyone else who wanted to listen that he'd been back home, talked to Mac, talked to Lou and there was nothing they could do to stop him. Roz had phoned Kirsty's mum, who'd put on her hurt look and accused Kirsty of lying so now Kirsty hadn't a clue which version she was supposed to give to Mrs Kershaw.

Should she mention the weird phone call? She hadn't even told her dad. She'd been so sure it was Jamie, being a prat. But if it wasn't Jamie, then who? Could it have been Mac? He knew her name, had seen their school uniforms, so he could have easily tried all the Broughtons in the area. There weren't that many in the phone book. But why should Mac want to warn her off Simon? Or could it have been Luke Harris, who just seemed to generally have it in for Simon? Simon himself, maybe? No logic behind that one, but then Simon's behaviour was barely ever logical, was it?

The office door opened and Sanjay came out, smirking. Lee and Tracy were told to go in together. Kirsty was left alone, her heart thudding alternately in her throat and her stomach while she told herself not to be so pathetic. She didn't have to say much. Just stick to basic apologies. It was only the Head of Year, not the Spanish Inquisition, for heaven's sake. Just how bad could it be?

Simon sat on a park bench, staring at the lake, wondering whether Kirsty would turn up. He didn't want to talk to her in school with teachers watching their every move, so he'd sent her a text, asking her to meet him here on her way home. She wasn't supposed to, he knew. According to Mrs Kershaw, Kirsty's parents hadn't been exactly pleased about her bunking off, getting mixed up with him, so she was supposed to keep her distance and maybe that's what she'd decided to do. He could hardly blame her.

He stood up, picked up a handful of stones, and started skimming them across the water. Paul had taught him to do that, on holiday in Wales, a couple of years after Simon had moved in with them. Then, at night, in the chalet, when he was supposed to be asleep, he'd heard them talking.

'Why does he do that?' Roz had whined at Paul. 'Why does he have to spoil everything? He could have blinded poor Ben!'

'He didn't mean to hit his eye,' Paul had said.

'He shouldn't have been throwing stones like that, in the first place,' Roz had insisted. 'The minute you turned your back on him, the minute you went to help Ellie with her sandcastle, he stopped skimming and started on Ben! It's like Simon wants all our attention, all of the time!'

'And can you blame him?' Paul had said. 'It's not as though he's ever had much, is it? I'm not sure those two even realised they had a kid, most of the time.'

'Kate did her best!'

'Oh, come off it, Roz! I know she was your sister but Kate never cared about anyone except herself. Not you, not Simon, not anyone.'

It wasn't true. It wasn't true. She did care. She loved

him. All the things Roz and Paul said, all the things he'd overheard them saying back then, all the things they'd told him last night, it was all lies, lies, lies. Simon whirled round, threw a large stone into a tree, heard a crow squawk and fly off, then Kirsty's voice.

'Simon! What the hell do you think you're doing?'

'Nothing!' he said. 'I didn't know the stupid bird was there, did I?'

'Simon, what is it? What's wrong?'

'Everything!' he said, slumping onto the bench, his head in his hands.

'Hey,' said Kirsty, sitting next to him.

'I don't want to know,' said Simon. 'I don't want to know.'

'Don't want to know what?' said Kirsty.

'Anything! I should never have started it. I shouldn't have asked. They're lying. They're all lying. She wasn't like that.'

He looked up, stared at Kirsty. What was she doing here? Why had he asked her to come? How could she help? How could anyone help? He stood up.

'Simon?' Kirsty said, as he began to walk away.

He carried on walking, ignoring her shout, hearing instead other voices, the voices from last night.

'What do you expect if you go digging around like that, Simon?' Roz had said. 'You're not gonna hear any good news, are you? Not from Lou, not from Mac, not from anybody.'

'So it was true, what he said about Mum?'

93

'Sort of,' Roz said. 'We tried to help. I tried. Paul tried. Maybe we should have tried harder. Kate was better, for a while ... when she first met your dad, when you were born but ... but then the bastard walked out on her, didn't he? And she went to pieces again, big time. Because he didn't just walk out and stay out, did he? Oh no, he kept coming back, stringing her along ...'

'They were both as bad,' Paul said, wearily. 'Neither of 'em knew what the hell they wanted. They were a mess, the pair of them. Him with his booze and his temper, her with her drugs.'

'I don't remember. I don't remember any of that!'

A middle-aged couple, arms linked, stopped for a moment to look at Simon. He'd been shouting out loud! No wonder they'd stared. No wonder they'd hurried off the other way. But it wasn't only their footsteps he could hear. There was another set, clopping towards him.

'Simon, wait,' Kirsty said.

He waited, let her catch up.

'I'm not going,' he said.

'Going where?'

'To see my dad again. Paul's right. What's the point? What's the point in stirring it all up again? It's doing my head in. Trying to think about it. Trying to work it out.'

'Maybe there isn't anything to work out,' said Kirsty.

'But if Mum was into all that stuff, it makes it more likely, doesn't it? That it could have been someone else. Not my dad. Some punter or dealer. Some random bloody burglar maybe. Who knows? The cops never looked into it properly. My dad told me that. But what does it matter? It's not gonna change anything, is it? It's not gonna bring her back. Even if I could remember something, even if I wanted to remember. I'm gonna burn them, when I get back. The letters, the newspaper articles. Everything.'

He'd meant to. He'd meant to burn them, even though Kirsty had told him not to do anything hasty, anything stupid, anything he'd regret. Instead, he'd got them out, read through the whole lot again. Checking his theory. It was funny, he'd thought, how well he could read when he wanted to, when it wasn't something for school. Maybe Jaz was right. Maybe he wasn't so thick, after all. Because he'd spotted something, there amongst the documents and newspaper reports, hadn't he? Or, at least he thought he had. He'd check it out with Kirsty. Kirsty was smart. She'd know if he was onto something or just seeing what he wanted to see.

Is that what he'd been doing all along? Seeing what he wanted to see? Selective memories? Blotting out the rest.

The papers were still scattered across the bedroom floor. He thought about picking them up but he was too tired. Too tired even to get undressed properly, so he just kicked off his shoes, wriggled out of his trousers and crawled under the duvet, still in his school shirt. Closed his eyes. Opened them again as he saw the waste ground, the sticks shoved into the soil, acting as goalposts. It was starting again. The dream. The same way it always started. Think of something. Something else. Anything else. Kirsty. Why not? Kirsty was safe. Harmless. Kirsty lying here on the bed with him. Imagine that. Kirsty holding him. Nothing else. Just holding him. Talking to him in that funny bossy sort of way she had. Talking to him, keeping the nightmares away.

Where are you? Where've you gone? Kirsty? Mum? I need a drink, Mum. Stumbling in the dark, on the stairs, falling but she doesn't hear. Nobody hears. Going into the kitchen. Milk. Standing on a chair to reach it. Gulping it down. All of it. Feeling sick 'cos it doesn't taste right. So horrible it makes me cry. Crying, trying to spit it out as I go back upstairs. Standing outside Mum's room. She doesn't like me to go in there. Not at night. Says she needs her sleep. But she's not asleep. I can hear her. I push open the door. See the bedside light on. Mum and Dad huddled together, breaking apart, her yelling at me, him sitting up. Not Dad. Dad doesn't live here now. Someone else, someone else, someone else. Someone without a face. A blank mask where the face ought to be. A plastic mask, melting, dripping while Mum leaps out of bed, rushes towards me, grabs my shoulders.

'Don't shout, Mum, don't do that, I didn't see anything, I didn't see, I'm sorry, leave me alone!'

'Leave me alone!'

The thud woke him. The thud of his own body rolling out of bed, crashing onto the floor. There were noises

96

outside too. People moving around. He looked at his clock. Quarter to eight already. Late. But that wasn't the worst thing. He scrambled up, grabbed a towel, and wrapped it round his waist, feeling sick as he glanced at the bed. Not again. It couldn't be. That didn't happen. Not anymore. Not for ages.

Simon snatched the duvet, tried to cover up the evidence as he heard the knock but it was too late. Dave was already in. Staring at Simon, staring at the bed, Dave's face never changing. No shock. No disapproval.

'Grab a shower,' Dave said, calmly. 'I'll deal with the rest.'

Simon wriggled into some old jogging bottoms. He opened the bedroom door intending to close it quickly and bolt to the shower room but he wasn't quite quick enough. Luke was there, peering past him, watching Dave pulling the sheet from the bed.

'You've wet the bed!' Luke yelped. 'You dirty bastard!'

'I didn't. I spilt a drink!'

'Simon's wet the bed,' Luke shouted. 'Simon's wet—'

He didn't get any further. Simon's fist smashed into his mouth, splitting his lip and before Luke could recover enough to retaliate, Dave was there, standing between them.

'Get Jaz to sort that out for you,' Dave snapped at Luke. 'Oh, and for the record, Luke, Simon was right. He spilt his drink, OK?'

*

'I don't get it,' Simon told Jaz later. 'It's years since I've done that! Years. I mean why should it start again? Now.'

They were sitting in the small 'visiting' lounge at Oakfields, waiting for Roz and Paul to turn up. Simon had been sick and worked himself into such a state that there was no way he could have gone to school. Dave had phoned Roz and, though Simon's aunt and uncle were the last people he wanted to see right now, they were on their way and there wasn't much he could do about it.

'It's not starting again,' Jaz was saying. 'It was a one-off, that's all. It happens, occasionally. To more people than you might think. Don't get uptight about it.'

'Oh, right,' said Simon. 'Sure! Like that helps! Like everybody believes the drink story, yeah? Like a split lip is gonna stop Luke mouthing off. Telling everyone. You should have seen the way he looked at me!'

'Dave'll deal with Luke,' Jaz said. 'You just concentrate on yourself, eh? Keeping calm is half the battle.'

'But I've been coping with the dreams,' said Simon, barely listening. 'Waking myself up in time to get to the loo. And it's not as though I even had the dream last night. Not *the* dream anyway. Not the bad one. It was another one. I was younger, I think, about four or five maybe...'

Jaz nodded as she listened to Simon's account of the dream.

'It's understandable enough,' said Jaz. 'After what that neighbour said, after what Roz and Paul told you. Dreams are just the brain sorting information.'

'The dreams I have don't feel like that,' said Simon. 'They feel like memories. And that bloke, with the melting face...it felt like I recognised him. Even though he had no features or nothing, it felt like I knew him. And it made me feel ill. Really ill.'

'So who—'

'I don't know,' said Simon. 'I didn't say I *really* recognised him, did I? I said it just felt like it. As though I *should* know him. As though it was important. Oh God, I think I'm going mad. I really think I'm going mad.'

'You're not mad, Simon,' said Jaz. 'Not even halfway there, I promise.'

'That therapy thing you told me about,' said Simon, abruptly. 'Do you really reckon it might help? I mean, would it help me remember stuff, properly?'

'Hypnotherapy?' said Jaz. 'It might do.'

'It's a load of rubbish, that, isn't it?' said Paul's voice from the doorway.

Simon looked up. How long had they been there, hovering, listening in? Had they heard him talking about the dream, the melting face? He hoped not. They thought he was crazy enough already without giving them more ammunition.

'How yer doin', mate?' Paul added, slapping Simon's shoulder, before following Roz to the sofa.

Simon didn't bother answering, partly because he didn't have a chance. Paul was still talking, addressing himself mainly to Roz.

'Yeah, I read about that hypnotherapy stuff. People go

to the doctor with unexplained headaches or insomnia or summat. Doctor recommends hypnotherapy and hey presto, while they're being regressed, the patient remembers being abused as a kid and some poor, usually male, relative gets put in gaol.'

'So they should if they've been abusing kiddies,' said Roz.

'That's the point though, innit?' said Paul. 'Half these cases turn out to be false memories, don't they? Ideas implanted by the therapist. Something the patient's seen on a film or something. There's no way of telling, see? What's real and what's not.'

'There have been a few problems,' said Jaz. 'But that wasn't quite what I was recommending for Simon.'

'He doesn't want to be bothered with any of it, do you, Si?' said Paul, fiddling with the small, gold loop in his left ear. 'May as well see a bloody witch doctor for all the good it'll do. Boil up a few chicken heads or make little wax dolls, eh?'

'I agree with Paul,' said Roz.

'No change there then,' Simon muttered.

'Don't be like that, Si,' said Paul. 'We just don't want you getting screwed up. I mean, it's not doing you any good, is it? All this dwelling on the past. Trying to change things you can't possibly change. However much you dig, you're not going to remember anything important because there isn't anything.'

'I don't like it any more than you do, Simon,' said Roz. 'But, how many times do we have to tell you?

There was no one else involved! Just your mum and your dad.'

'You don't know that,' said Simon. 'You can't be sure. There's things. Other things.'

'Dreams don't mean anything,' Paul said.

So they *had* heard all that! Great, just great.

'I'm not talking about the dreams!' Simon snapped.

'Well, I hope you haven't been taking too much notice of Lou,' said Roz. ' 'Cos she's away with the fairies, she is. Couldn't even see what them stepsons of hers were doing right under her fat nose. Still thinks they're the bees' bloody knees, from what I can make out. And that Mac's just a sleazy old git. Wouldn't trust him if my life depended on it.'

'It's not anything *they* said,' Simon began.

He stopped, decided not to mention what he'd found out. Not until he'd had a chance to show Kirsty. It would probably turn out to be nothing and he didn't want to make himself look an idiot in front of Jaz.

'It's just that I think I've buried a lot of stuff. Stuff about my mum that I didn't want to know. But maybe I've buried something important as well.'

'You haven't!' said Roz. 'How many times do we have to tell you!'

'Anyway, that's not really the issue,' said Jaz, ignoring the scowls from Roz and Paul. 'It's not necessarily about retrieving *important* memories; it's about Simon being able to resolve things. Regression sometimes helps to release some of the anger.'

'Sounds like he released a fair bit on that Luke this morning,' said Paul.

'And that's what we want to avoid, right?' said Jaz. 'I know you've tried to protect Simon but, in the long term, you might not have done him any favours. At some point he's got to face everything. Not avoid it. Face it.'

'He's not facing it though, is he?' said Roz. 'He's living in a fantasy land. One where his dad's innocent and his mum's some sort of bloody saint.'

'Well that's exactly what the therapy is about,' said Jaz. 'Helping him to come to terms with reality. Whatever that reality turns out to be. However hard it is to deal with.'

'So how long would it take to fix up?' said Simon, as Roz shook her head. 'When can I start?'

Chapter 9

Kirsty didn't know exactly where Oakfields was so after school she looked out for Briony and followed, at a distance. Kirsty wasn't sure why she hadn't approached Briony directly and asked to walk with her but, somehow, everything involving Simon drove her to subterfuge, made her nervous, cautious. Though not quite cautious enough to make her pull away from him.

She'd got his text message earlier in the day. Not only wasn't he going to be in school but he'd been grounded for thumping Luke again, so could she come to Oakfields. She hadn't, of course, told her parents she was making a diversion and, as they weren't due home for a couple of hours, they'd never know, would they?

Ignoring Simon's message, refusing his request, hadn't really crossed Kirsty's mind. Sure the weird phone call, warning her off him, was a bit worrying but it couldn't be serious. No one could actually stop her seeing Simon if she wanted to.

Kirsty paused, looked round, realised she couldn't see Briony anymore. She must have gone down the side street on the left, a bit further along. As Kirsty hurried on, she had the sudden feeling that someone was watching her. Simon's paranoia must be catching, she told herself but she couldn't resist glancing back. There were two people, a fair distance behind. Two men.

A white van, with writing on the side, drove past, splashing her legs with mud and, as she bent automatically to wipe them with her hand, the men seemed to quicken their pace. Probably nothing but Kirsty wasn't taking any chances. She straightened up, darted round the corner and caught up with Briony, who was walking slowly up the hill, as if it was a massive effort.

'What you doing round here?' Briony asked, the sulky expression on her sharp, pale face indicating that she already knew.

'Going to see Simon,' Kirsty muttered, looking back to see the two men turning into the street.

'You OK?' Briony asked.

'I think there's a couple of men following me,' whispered Kirsty. 'Don't look!'

It was too late, Briony had already checked.

'Yeah, well they would be, wouldn't they?' she said. 'It's Dave and Al. They work at Oakfields. They've been up at the school this afternoon, I think. Hey!' she called back to them. 'Kirsty thinks you're a couple of stalkers!'

Briony amused herself shouting out to Dave and Al until they reached Oakfields, where, mercifully, Simon was waiting in the foyer.

'Come on,' he said to Kirsty. 'I've got something to show you.'

'I bet you have!' mumbled Briony, walking off.

'I was gonna give up on all this,' said Simon, ushering

Kirsty into his room, where piles of paper littered his bed and the floor. 'But I just want you to have a look at this first. See what you think.'

He pushed away some of the papers, making room for them to sit down on the end of the bed, then picked up a notepad.

'I've written down what Mac said at the time, look. He said he heard the shouts at about 8:15 and that I came running out onto the street, screaming, at about half past.'

'Well, that sort of fits with what he told us, doesn't it?' said Kirsty. 'He said eightish or half past.'

'Yeah,' said Simon. 'But that can't be right, see. 'Cos I remember I didn't leave my mates till nearly nine o'clock.'

'Hold on,' said Kirsty. 'It was nearly ten years ago. You were only seven! How can you possibly remember?'

'I'm not lying!'

'I didn't say you were! I just mean the memory might not be real, accurate. Like not remembering your house properly.'

'It is though,' said Simon. 'I know it is. 'Cos I had a new watch and I was, like, really proud of being able to tell the time. And when I first looked I thought I must have got it wrong 'cos I was ages late. I was supposed to be in by half past seven! So I looked again, even said it out to myself. Little hand on nine, big hand almost at the top. That's how I knew how late I was.'

'But you must have told the cops, at the time, yes?'

'I don't know. I don't think so. Maybe they didn't ask. Would they expect a kid like me to know the time? Would they care? Or was it like my dad said? They thought they had their man and didn't bother looking. 'Cos think about it, Kirsty, if Mac really heard shouting at 8:15 but I didn't see Dad leave the house till gone nine...I mean would Dad have hung around for three quarters of an hour after he'd, if he'd—'

'No,' said Kirsty. 'He wouldn't. But we don't know whether Mac got any of it right, do we? People get confused about time. It might not mean anything. Maybe he had his own reasons for lying. Nothing sinister, just his own reasons.'

'But is it worth me mentioning?' said Simon, almost desperately. 'To the cops or Dad's solicitor or someone.'

'Probably,' said Kirsty. 'Can't do any harm. Just don't get your hopes up too much, that's all.'

'No chance of that,' said Simon. ''Cos it's gonna be bad, whichever way it turns out, innit?'

'What do you mean?'

'Either he's guilty, which is bad enough, yeah? But if they re-opened the case, found out it wasn't him, then that's even worse, in a way. 'Cos he's spent ten years in gaol for something he didn't do. Ten years! He was twenty-eight when they put him away. He's the same age as Uncle Paul but Dad looks about fifty now. Worn down, worn-out, screwed-up. I mean, how do you give someone ten years of their life back? You can't, can you?'

Kirsty hadn't thought of it like that. Sure she'd seen cases on the news sometimes. Miscarriages of justice. But she'd never really thought about how it must feel, what it did to you, to lose years of your life like that. Years you could have spent with your friends, your family. The anger, the bitterness, gnawing away at you. No amount of compensation could make up for it.

'You may as well look at the rest of the stuff, while you're here,' said Simon. 'If that's OK? See if there's anything else that might be important.'

'Sure,' said Kirsty, beginning to read through the articles. 'But should you be doing this? I mean, stirring everything up, time after time.'

'I'm OK.'

How could he say that, when it was even upsetting her to read it? His mum was only twenty-five when she died. Eighteen then, when Simon was born. And the more Kirsty read, the more obvious it seemed that Simon's dad was guilty, that there was no one else involved. Yet all the time she was reading, Simon kept imagining scenarios, putting forward other possibilities: Mac, those step-sons of Lou's, a random psychopath, the drug dealers, even some faceless punter Simon had dreamt about!

'It's not really the business with the times,' Simon was saying. 'Or anything solid. It's more of a feeling. Like I said to Roz and Paul, it's as though I've got something locked away inside me, telling me it wasn't Dad. Something that's buried, that I can't bring out. You think that's nuts, don't you?'

'Er, no,' said Kirsty. 'Not really.'

'Thanks,' said Simon. 'You sound really sure about that! Anyway, that's why I've agreed to this hypnotherapy stuff. Just in case it brings something back. Trouble is, it'll probably screw me up again, Jaz says. In the short term, at least. So you'll have to watch out for me. Make sure I don't do anything too freaky, eh?'

He'd taken hold of her hand, leant towards her as he was talking but suddenly he pulled back and stood up.

'It's almost six. You'd better go,' he said. 'Before your mum and dad get back.'

'Yeah,' said Kirsty, standing up, walking over to the window, and looking out onto the already dusky street.

'Something wrong?'

'No, not really,' said Kirsty. 'I've just been getting a bit spooked since the phone call on Wednesday night.'

'What phone call?'

'Didn't I tell you?'

Simon shook his head, frowning as she started to explain.

'That's funny,' he said. ''Cos I've had a couple of weird texts. I sort of thought it was Luke, winding me up... but... what if it's not? What if someone's trying to scare me? Stop me asking questions?'

'How could it be?' said Kirsty. 'How would anyone know your mobile number?'

'Well I gave it to Lou. So I guess she could have passed it on.'

'Simon,' said Kirsty, as a sudden thought struck her. 'Have you been talking to anyone else? Apart from Lou and Mac?'

'A few, yeah,' said Simon. 'Quite a lot, I suppose. I mean Lou's bloke Ian was around, when I went to see her. Then there were some people Lou put me onto. No one important. Just people who knew my mum.'

'And did you give out your number to any of them?'

'I might have done, yeah. You know, in case they suddenly remembered something and—'

'Don't!' said Kirsty. 'Don't say anymore! It's giving me the creeps just thinking about it.'

'Sorry,' said Simon. 'Tell you what, I'll walk back with you, eh? Save me sitting around here bored out of my head.'

'You can't,' said Kirsty. 'You're grounded, remember?'

'Yeah,' said Simon. 'But Briony's taught me a little trick with the laundry room window. If you go out the front, I'll meet you down the road.'

'No, don't,' said Kirsty. 'You'll only be in trouble again when they find out.'

'They probably won't,' said Simon. 'I've already told 'em I'd make myself a sandwich and not bother with dinner tonight, in case Luke starts summat in the dining room. And even if they notice I'm missing, what difference does it make? I'm out of here soon, aren't I?'

As Kirsty made her way out, she wondered how Simon could be so casual about trouble. She hated it, would go a million miles to avoid it, usually. The ten minutes or so she'd spent with Killer Kershaw had been agony, even though there'd been no repercussions, no detention, just a warning against mixing with 'the wrong sort of people'.

Was Simon 'the wrong sort'? Kirsty's parents thought so, but then they didn't really know him, did they? They only knew what they'd heard. Judged and condemned him on that. Simon wasn't bad. Just screwed-up. And, after what she'd just read, it was hardly surprising, was it? It was a miracle he had any sort of sanity left at all.

She walked a few paces down the road, away from prying eyes, and waited but there was no sign of him. Had he been caught on his way out? She waited a few minutes longer, decided he must have been and moved on. As she reached the corner, she heard him running to catch up.

'Sorry,' said Simon. 'I got out OK, then had the bright idea to bring my bike so I could cycle back to Oakfields but when I wheeled it out of the shed, it had a puncture. I think the chain might be knackered as well. I ought to get it all fixed up. I'm good at that sort of thing, Paul says. Practical stuff. I used to help him with his van and doing bits of jobs around the house. Ben and Ellie were never interested.'

'They're both younger than you are, right?'

'Thirteen and nine. Ellie was just a baby when I moved in, so it couldn't have been a bundle of fun for Roz and Paul, could it?' he said, smiling at her. 'With two young kids and a nutter like me.'

'You're not a nutter!'

'Thanks but let's just say I wasn't easy,' said Simon. 'Luckily Ben and Ellie were. They're both quiet, swotty types...like you!'

'Hey,' said Kirsty, lightly punching his arm. 'You don't know anything about me.'

'No, I don't, do I?' said Simon, thoughtfully. 'It's always me we talk about, isn't it? So, you've got about fifteen minutes, I guess, to tell me all about you.'

'I won't even need fifteen seconds,' said Kirsty. 'There's nothing much to tell. I'm just, well, pretty ordinary really.'

'No, you're not ordinary,' said Simon. 'Definitely not ordinary.'

The intensity of his voice made her shiver, caught her unawares, prevented her from speaking.

'So,' he said, more sharply. 'Tell me about you and Jamie.'

Jamie! That was over, done with, finished. No way was she going out with someone who'd dumped on her like that! He'd tried to wheedle round her at afternoon registration and she'd told him where to go but she wasn't sure she was quite ready to share that information with Simon. Especially not all the stuff Jamie had said about him!

'Er, I'd rather not,' said Kirsty. 'I'll tell you about my family instead, shall I? Starting with my nephew, Henry...he's a bit of a character.'

By the time they turned into Kirsty's street, she'd rattled through the family, with just one more to go.

'Last but not least, there's Monty,' she said.

'Monty?'

'My pet rat.'

'A rat!' said Simon. 'You keep a rat! Yuk.'

'That's what Dad says. So I have to keep him in the bedroom...Monty, not my dad!'

'Remind me,' said Simon, leaning on her gate. 'Never to come into your bedroom.'

'I wasn't going to invite you,' said Kirsty, knowing her eyes were giving another message entirely, knowing his were giving the same message in response.

He was going to kiss her, she was sure. She ought to move away. Her parents might drive up at any moment. Oh, to hell with her parents. She edged forward, sliding her arms round Simon's waist, letting her lips find his. But it wasn't the long, lingering kiss she'd been expecting. Suddenly Simon was pushing her away; almost jumping back as though she'd bitten him.

'Sorry,' he said, yet there was no apology in his tone, only anger.

Anger reflected in the way he hurried off, not once glancing back at her.

'Damn!' said Kirsty, as she headed up the path.

How could she have been so stupid? How could she have misread the signals, like that? Trying to kiss him when that was probably the last thing on his mind, when his head was probably still full of his dad, his mum, all the stuff they'd been reading over back at Oakfields. How could she have been so insensitive? Or maybe it was nothing to do with any of that. Maybe he just didn't fancy her. Why should he?

She stormed round the house, automatically doing all the jobs she usually did when she came in, shoving the dinner in the microwave, instead of in the oven to save time, so everything was ready when her parents turned up. There were no suspicions, no questions about her being late; just a couple about why she was so quiet.

'Tired,' she muttered, as she helped her parents clear away. 'Think I'll just finish my homework and have an early night.'

She was getting her books out when the doorbell rang.

'I'll go,' she said, wearily. 'It's probably Jamie. He's having trouble understanding the word no.'

She opened the door, venom ready on her lips but it wasn't Jamie, it was Simon.

'Oh my God!' she said.

'Kirsty, I—'

His face was bruised, his forehead grazed and as he leant against the doorpost, he seemed to shrink. Not shrinking. Sliding. Sliding down almost to his knees, the light from the hall showing clearly the red patch seeping through his hoody.

'Oh, Simon, no,' Kirsty hissed, glancing back into the house. 'Not again. Not here! Not now. Simon, stop it. Get up. This isn't funny. This is—'

Different. Not like before. Fake blood not on his chest this time. On his face, on his back. High up. To the right. Right shoulder.

'Simon,' she said again, bending down, trying to lift him. 'Simon?'

She saw the rip in his hoody, the tear in the shirt beneath, the gash in his flesh. Not fake this time. The gash, the blood, was real.

'Mum!' she screamed as Simon suddenly fell from her grip and slumped face down on the floor.

Chapter 10

'You've got a visitor,' said the nurse, on Sunday afternoon as she closed the curtains round Simon's bed. 'But I just want to change your drip first.'

'It's not the cops again, is it? Wanting to know if I'm involved in drugs and gang warfare?'

'No, it's the girl who came in with you on Friday night. Christie?'

'Kirsty,' said Simon, sitting up. 'Her name's Kirsty. Are you gonna be long with that thing?'

He'd had dozens of visitors already. At least he guessed so by the number of cards littering the bedside table and hazy memories of curious faces peering at him but all the conversations were a bit of a blur. He vaguely remembered talking to Roz and Paul that morning but he'd been half asleep so they'd left, threatening to come back later.

'Done!' said the nurse, whipping back the curtains.

Simon saw Kirsty hovering by the doorway. She hurried over to him as the nurse left, sat in the chair beside the bed and pulled something from her bag.

'Chocolates,' she said, adding her offering to the pile already on the table. 'Sorry, didn't know what else to bring. How you feeling?'

'Dunno,' said Simon. 'I'm so doped up on painkillers I can't feel anything much.'

'They say it's not serious,' said Kirsty.

'Oh, that's all right then,' said Simon. 'Some psycho tries to kill me but it's not serious.'

'You know what I mean,' said Kirsty. 'Your face isn't exactly pretty but the stab wound's only surface and there's no damage to any vital organs or anything. You were lucky.'

'Sure. Lucky's my middle name. You can tell by the charmed life I've led, can't you?'

He knew he was whingeing, wrapping himself in a blanket of self-pity but he couldn't help it.

'The police came round to talk to me yesterday,' Kirsty was saying.

'Why?'

'Just to check a few things but I told them about going to see Mac and everything.'

'Why?' said Simon. 'What d'yer do that for?'

'I thought I should. In case it turned out to be important.'

'It won't! It's got nothing to do with any of that. I've already told 'em who did it!'

'I know but Luke's denying it,' said Kirsty. 'Says he never left Oakfields on Friday.'

'Yeah, well he would, wouldn't he? But I bet he can't prove it.'

'Maybe not,' said Kirsty. 'But you can't prove anything either, can you?'

'No but it's obvious, innit? I get back to Oakfields and

Luke's there, staring at me out of his window, sticking his finger up so I decide not to bother going in.'

'You go to the park, instead?'

'Yeah,' said Simon. 'And don't bother looking at me like that 'cos I wasn't gonna do nothing freaky with ketchup, OK? Anyway, he follows me, doesn't he?'

'Maybe,'said Kirsty. 'But you don't actually see him?'

'Have we had this conversation before?' Simon asked.

'Sort of,' said Kirsty. 'You tried to tell us on Friday night, while we were waiting for the ambulance but you weren't exactly coherent and I don't think I really took it all in.'

'So,' said Simon. 'I was just wandering round, thinking about stuff till I got desperate for a pee. I mean I even looked round before I went in the loo, in case there were any of those pervy types you get hanging around. But there wasn't. There wasn't anyone till I came out, then smack! Someone slams my face against the toilet wall and I get this sharp pain in my back. Will you stop looking at me like that!'

'Like what?'

'Like you don't believe me. Like you think I did it to myself or summat.'

'I'm not accusing you of stabbing yourself!' said Kirsty. 'You'd have to be a bit of a contortionist for a start, to reach back there. And I do believe you. I'm just not sure it's Luke that's all. The cops still think it might have been a random mugging. With your wallet and phone missing and everything but—'

'But what? Oh shit,' he added, staring past her up the ward.

Kirsty turned to see two people walking towards them.

'Paul and Roz,' said Simon.

'I'll go,' said Kirsty.

'No, don't,' he said, as they approached.

He tried not to cringe as Roz hugged him and gushed at Kirsty as if they were old friends.

'Just thought we'd pop in,' said Paul, hovering by the bed. 'Can't stay long though, mate. Got a job to do. Some old dear's got a bunged-up pipe. But we'll come back and see you again tonight.'

'Don't bother,' said Simon.

Paul laughed and winked at Kirsty.

'He doesn't mean it,' Paul said. 'Do you, Si? Anyway, we've got some good news for you.'

'The cops have arrested Luke?' said Simon.

'No,' said Roz, wearily. 'And they're not going to. He's got alibis. People who were with him at Oakfields.'

'Amrit and Ricky, yeah?' said Simon.

'Yes,' said Roz. 'How did you know?'

'It's obvious, innit? Amrit's his bloody lap-dog and Luke could scare Ricky into agreeing to anything.'

'But why would Luke want to stab you?' said Roz.

'He don't like me,' said Simon.

'There's loads of people I don't like,' said Roz. 'But I don't go around attacking them!'

'Yeah, well you're not a psycho,' said Simon. 'Luke

is. Attacked his step-dad with a hammer, Briony says. Fractured the bloke's skull! That's why Luke ended up in care.'

'Care!' said Paul. 'I'm surprised he wasn't locked up.'

'He was only nine at the time,' said Simon. 'And, according to Briony, the step-dad and Luke's mum had been beating the shit out of him for years, so maybe the cops thought the step-dad deserved it. I dunno, do I?'

'Are you sure this Briony's got her facts right?' said Roz. 'I mean, if Luke was that dangerous, he wouldn't be at Oakfields, would he? Or in an ordinary school?'

'He wasn't, at first. He was in some sort of secure unit but they reckoned he was safe enough to be let out. And the only thing he's attacked with a weapon since then is a bit of furniture,' said Simon. 'Till now.'

'I don't know,' said Kirsty. 'It doesn't make any sense. I know you and Luke have had punch-ups but actually following you and stabbing you? That's way different, isn't it? I mean, let's just say it wasn't Luke. And let's say it wasn't a random mugging thing either. What if it's got something to do with the questions you've been asking? I mean, it's a bit of a co-incidence, isn't it? The creepy phone calls and now this?'

'Read a lot of thrillers, do you?' said Roz, smiling.

Kirsty was about to admit that she did, when Paul spoke.

'No, hang on,' he said. 'She could be right, I suppose. Maybe Simon's really got on to something.'

'Oh, don't you start, Paul!' said Roz. 'To believe that,

you'd have to believe there was something to cover up, wouldn't you? And there isn't!'

'I don't know,' said Kirsty. 'Simon reckons there's something dodgy about what Mac said about the time of the—'

'I'd be surprised if Mac could tell the flaming time,' said Roz.

'But if Simon's right?' said Paul, thoughtfully.

Simon looked at his uncle. Kirsty buying the conspiracy theory was one thing, but Paul? What was he up to?

'That was probably nothing, anyway,' Simon muttered. 'Just me getting the memories all twisted again.'

'Well,' said Paul, to his wife, 'one thing's for sure. We don't want nothing like this happening again, do we? So, you'd better tell him, eh?'

'Is this the good news you were on about?' Simon asked.

'Yeah,' said Roz. 'Paul and me have been talking and we want you to come home. They obviously can't look after you proper at Oakfields. At least if you were home, we'd know you were safe. Especially after what you've just said about Luke.'

'Oh, right,' said Simon, glaring at Paul. 'So that's what it's all about, is it? Come home, so you can keep an eye on me! Stop me asking questions, stop me going to see my dad!'

'That's not what we meant!' Roz protested. 'We thought you'd be pleased.'

'Yeah, well thanks but no thanks. I'm staying at

Oakfields. For a start I'm not gonna let Luke Harris think he's won. I'm not scared of him no matter how many knives and hammers he's got!'

'It's all right,' said Paul, touching his wife's arm, as she started to protest again. 'Whatever you want, Si. But you're going to have to be a bit more careful, OK? Stay away from Luke. And definitely keep away from Mac and all that stuff! Leave it to the cops, eh?'

'Like they listen, yeah?'

'They'll maybe listen to me,' said Paul. 'Tell me what you've been up to, who you've seen, what you think you've found out and I'll talk to 'em, right? I'll even go and see your dad's solicitor, if that's what you want. How's that?'

'Er, thanks,' said Simon, prompted by a glance from Kirsty.

'Yeah, well,' said Paul. 'Nothing's gonna stop you going on about it, so the sooner we try and get it sorted the better, eh?'

'You're not supposed to have that on in here,' Roz said, as Paul's phone rang.

He switched it off without answering.

'Mrs Burton,' he said. 'She'll be wanting to know why I'm not round there unbunging her pipe. Better go.'

'They seem nice,' said Kirsty, as she watched Roz and Paul walk back up the ward.

'Suppose they are,' said Simon. 'In their own little way. When you don't have to live with them!'

*

121

Kirsty wasn't sure Simon had made the right decision about going back to Oakfields but it seemed to have worked out all right so far, she thought, as she got out of Mum's car and hobbled up the drive towards the care home. It was early days yet though. Simon had been let out of hospital on Thursday and Luke, according to Briony, had been hastily moved to a foster home. Obviously not very far away though because he was still in school, which might be tricky when Simon came back. If he came back. When Kirsty had popped in after school, on Friday, Paul had been there, coaxing, cajoling, trying to get Simon to move back with them and it had seemed as though Simon might have been weakening, especially as Paul had done as promised, talking to the cops and the solicitor.

'They don't hold out much hope,' Paul had said. 'But at least they listened and they're looking in to it.'

Kirsty hadn't stayed long, partly because Paul had seemed keen to talk to Simon on his own and partly because she'd arranged to go bowling with Sonja and a couple of friends, in an attempt to get back to some sort of normality. It had been a bit of a disaster not least because Jamie had pestered her with texts every ten minutes and, even worse, her friends had taken his side.

'Go on, answer him,' Sonja had said. 'He's desperate to get back with you. He told me!'

'Jamie wants what he can't have,' Kirsty had snapped. 'He's like a spoilt kid. Pathetic.'

'He just can't understand why you prefer Simon

Wells to him!' Sonja had said, as Kirsty prepared to hurl a bowl down the alley. 'And to be honest, neither can I. I mean at least Jamie's fairly sane!'

Kirsty had swung round, dropped the heavy bowl on her foot and screamed. There was nothing broken, the doctor had said on Saturday morning, it was just a bit bruised and swollen. Well, she could see that, couldn't she? It was still throbbing now, despite the painkillers and spending the whole of Saturday 'resting' it, as Mum had insisted. Mum had wanted her to rest today too and hadn't been exactly thrilled when Kirsty announced her intention of seeing Simon but eventually Mum had given in.

'All right, I'll take you,' Mum had said. 'But once he's better, that's it. I don't want you involved with him, Kirsty. There's been nothing but trouble...'

The lecture had gone on for the whole journey. Kirsty hadn't argued but then she hadn't exactly agreed to anything either.

Reaching the front of the home, Kirsty stopped, shifted her weight onto her right foot, pressed the buzzer and spoke into the intercom. Jaz opened the door.

'Simon's out the back,' Jaz said, smiling. 'Down the corridor, door on the left, past the laundry room. Should be open, they're all out there.'

Kirsty could see why Simon liked Jaz, why she was the only care worker he had any time for. She was sort of natural and friendly. Not intimidating at all.

The garden was bigger than Kirsty had expected. It

was a warm day, more like spring than autumn, and a group of lads were playing football with Al. Simon though was over by the sheds, fixing his bike with Paul. Briony was sprawled out on a bench, watching them, stretching out her hand every so often to try and catch the leaves that were drifting from the trees.

'What's wrong with your foot?' Simon asked as Kirsty approached.

'Bowling,' said Kirsty, deciding not to go into detail. 'Dangerous sport! Talking of which, are you going to ride that thing? I mean, shouldn't it have two wheels?'

'It will have in a minute,' said Simon. 'And a new chain. You don't mind if we carry on, do you? I want to get it done for school tomorrow.'

'Tomorrow?' said Kirsty, perching on the arm of the bench, as Briony showed no indication of wanting to make room for her. 'Are you sure you're fit enough to go at all, let alone ride a bike?'

'Yeah,' said Simon. 'Got to be, haven't I, 'cos I'm going to see my dad on Wednesday. They won't let me go if I don't make an effort to get back to school, will they? Then on Friday I've got my first hypnotherapy thing at the clinic.'

'Oooooo,' said Paul, swinging a bit of broken bike chain in front of Simon's face. 'You are feeling sleeeeepy.'

'Geroff!' said Simon. 'Jaz says it's not like that!'

'It's a load of mumbo-jumbo claptrap,' said Paul,

suddenly serious. 'That's going to get you all screwed up again.'

'Yeah well, I'll try anything once,' said Simon, turning towards Kirsty.

Kirsty saw Paul shaking his head.

'Don't suppose there's been any news from the solicitor or anything?' Kirsty asked, trying to divert them from another full-scale row about therapy.

'Solicitor?' said Paul. 'Er, no. These things take ages. You need to make that nut a bit tighter, Si. Use the other spanner. That's right.'

It wasn't exactly enthralling watching Simon cleaning, oiling and assembling various bike bits and attempts to talk to Briony got only mumbled responses, so after an hour Kirsty phoned her mum. Simon, Kirsty thought, as she turned out of Oakfields, had barely noticed her leave.

Paul's van was parked outside Oakfields but there was no sign of Mum. Kirsty looked at the van for a moment before limping down the hill to meet Mum at the bottom. About halfway down, she noticed a lad in a red baseball cap walking or rather slouching towards her. Luke Harris! What was he doing hanging around? Kirsty put her head down determined not to look at him but, at the last minute, as they were about to pass each other, she couldn't resist a glance.

'What you looking at?' he said, standing right in front of her. 'I'm allowed to walk up a street you know. Not on bloody curfew, am I? I'm meeting Amrit, if you want to know.'

125

Kirsty didn't. Not really. She didn't want to know anything about Luke Harris. What Simon had told her was quite enough! She'd always avoided Luke in school, even before she knew his background. There was something about him that made her almost shudder. It was like facing a wall of solid anger. A wall he'd probably been building for sixteen years.

'Right,' she said, edging past. 'OK. See ya.'

She didn't dare look back until she reached the end of the road and Mum's car swung round the corner, and when Kirsty checked, Luke had gone. Had he gone into Oakfields? Would he kick off with Simon again? At least there were plenty of staff around, not to mention Simon's uncle. Paul seemed a nice enough bloke, but he was fairly big, solid, not the kind of guy you messed with. She doubted that even Luke would have a go at Simon, with Paul protecting him.

As he set off for school on Monday morning, Simon slung his bag on his shoulders, yelped as it banged against his injury, and took it off again. He hooked it over the handlebars of his bike. Roz would go mad if she saw it. She was paranoid about safety. She'd even bought him a helmet, when she'd turned up with Ben and Ellie, late yesterday afternoon, after Kirsty had gone, just as Luke was being escorted off the premises.

Before Luke could even think about causing any bother, his foster carers had been called to take him home and Simon couldn't resist going up to his room to watch out of the window. Having seen Luke safely removed, Simon had shoved the helmet under his bed, where it could stay. No way was he going to wear it. He'd look a right wimp, wouldn't he, with Briony, Amrit and a couple of the others, standing round, watching as though they'd never seen a bike before.

'See ya at school then,' he said, getting onto the bike.

'If it makes it,' said Amrit.

Simon ignored him, pedalling out of the drive, through the open gate onto the road. He wasn't exactly keen on going back to school but, if he had to go, cycling was definitely better than walking with Briony gibbering in his ear, or being delivered by one of the care workers. He took his feet off the pedals, freewheeling, picking up speed. Something else Roz wouldn't approve of. But it was safe enough; he could see the junction at the bottom with the early morning traffic crawling past. Plenty of time to brake. In fact, now would be good.

He lightly touched the back brake. Nothing happened. He did it again, harder this time. Still nothing. There was no grip. None at all. He couldn't believe it. The bike was careering out of control towards the busy junction. What was he supposed to do? Veer into the kerb, towards the parked cars, the hedges, the walls, all flashing past in a blur? Or keep going, keep pressing, keep hoping? He tried stretching his legs out, letting his feet touch the ground in a desperate attempt to stop but it was too late. He was shooting out of the junction right in front of a car.

Chapter 11

Simon heard the squeal of car brakes as his feet finally jammed onto the road, jolting his whole body, sending pain ripping through his ribs, his back, his shoulders. His feet were burning, tearing, as the bike swerved and juddered. His fingers closed on the front brakes causing the bike to lurch, hurling him forward. His body smashed onto the bonnet of a car and, as he rolled off onto the road, he knew he was going to die.

'Bloody idiot came right out in front of me. What the hell did he think he was doing?'

'Is he all right?'

'Call an ambulance. Somebody call an ambulance!'

'I already have. Don't touch him. Don't try to move him!'

Not dead then. He didn't feel exactly conscious but he must be because he could hear the voices. Dozens of them all at once. He could sense people around him, leaning over him but he couldn't see them. Why couldn't he see them? He tried to put his hand up to his eyes but it wouldn't move. Nothing would move. He couldn't feel his limbs. He couldn't feel anything. No pain now. Nothing. That couldn't be right. Even the voices were fading, slipping away from him. He tried to hang on, stay with it but it was no good. Everything was slipping away.

'The bike was just like this tangled heap. All twisted and scrunched up,' Briony was saying. 'And I thought he was dead. I really thought he was dead.'

'He was lucky,' said Amrit. 'I mean if the traffic had been moving fast. If the car had hit him full on.'

Kirsty leant against the wall, trying to force herself to breathe properly, trying to take it all in, fighting back the sickness that had been with her all morning. There was still no real news. Kirsty had phoned the hospital herself at the start of lunch but all they'd say was that Simon was 'comfortable'. What the hell did that mean? How could he possibly be comfortable?

'He must have done it on purpose,' said Briony.

'What?' said Kirsty.

'The way he went down that hill,' said Briony. 'Like a bloody maniac, like he had no intention of stopping.'

'Bollocks,' said Amrit. 'Simon's a bit of a head-case but he's not suicidal, is he? His brakes must have failed, that's all.'

'How can they have done?' said Briony. 'I watched him tighten them myself.'

'Bollocks,' said Amrit again. 'You wouldn't know a brake pad from a bloody rhinoceros, you wouldn't.'

'Maybe not,' said Briony. 'But that uncle of his was standing over him all afternoon, making sure he did everything proper. Checking and double-checking. You saw him, didn't you, Kirsty?'

Kirsty nodded.

'So what happened when they'd finished?' said Kirsty. 'Where did he keep the bike overnight?'

'Well he mucked about on it for a bit till it got dark, then put it in the shed,' said Amrit. 'Why?'

'And is the shed locked?' said Kirsty.

'No,' said Amrit. 'No point. The side gate's locked, so no one can get out the back 'cept through the house or over the wall and the wall's massive, innit? So what you saying, anyway? That someone knackered his bike deliberate or summat?'

'No,' said Kirsty. 'I just wondered, that's all.'

'Either of you got any credit on your phones?' Briony asked.

'Yeah,' said Kirsty. 'Why?'

'Hand it over,' said Briony. 'And I'll phone Oakfields. See if anyone knows how he is.'

Simon opened his eyes. The curtain and the faces peering at him seemed sort of familiar.

'Didn't expect to see you back here so soon,' said the nurse, as the two blurred faces Simon was looking at merged into one. 'No, don't try and move. At least not quickly. You've got a bit of concussion.'

'I'm going to be sick,' said Simon.

The nurse shoved a cardboard bowl in front of him and, as he leant forward, pain ripped across his shoulders, down his back.

'Oh God!' he said.

From being able to feel nothing out on the road, he could now feel everything. Every bit of him was churning, burning, aching, throbbing. He groaned as he vomited into the bowl, the effort exhausting him, forcing tears as he flopped back against the pillow.

'I'm sorry,' he said, looking down, suddenly aware of his left arm, which was hooked in a sling across his chest.

'You broke it,' said the nurse. 'But apart from that, all the bruising and the slight concussion, you're fine. It's amazing how well people bounce at your age!'

'Yeah, right!'

'Your aunt and uncle are with the doctor, by the way. They'll be through to see you in a minute. And I'll get you some more painkillers. You look as though you might need them.'

'You could say that. My face feels a right mess. I've got bruises on top of bruises I reckon.'

'Your face isn't the problem,' said the nurse. 'It'll heal quickly enough. It's internal injuries you have to watch. How's your head now? Can you remember what happened?'

'Sort of,' said Simon. 'I remember the ambulance. I don't remember getting into it but I remember being lifted out...yeah and being pushed round on a trolley. But everything was spinning like being on one of them whirly things at the fair or summat. I still feel sort of dizzy.'

'Well, I can give you something for that and it'll take a bit of the sickness away as well, OK?'

Simon tried to smile as she left but even that hurt, so he closed his eyes, tried to concentrate on keeping everything totally still. But the sudden darkness made the dizziness worse and he felt as though he was back on the bike again, picking up speed, heading towards the cars, the brakes spinning. He opened his eyes, just as the curtains parted and the nurse re-appeared with his tablets.

'The bike,' he said. 'What's happened to the bike?'

'Not sure,' said the nurse. 'Why?'

'I want to know what happened,' said Simon. 'I want to know why the brakes failed.'

As Kirsty left the dining room on Tuesday lunchtime, she noticed Jamie abandon his lunch and follow her outside. They hadn't sat together or even spoken much since he'd dumped on her the day she'd bunked off with Simon and Kirsty was quite happy to keep it that way. She couldn't be doing with Jamie right now.

'Hey!' he said, as she limped towards the music block.

'I can't stop,' she said. 'I've got my clarinet lesson.'

'I'll walk with you.'

'Don't bother,' she said but she couldn't help smiling at the way he was loping along beside her, doing an exaggerated limp.

'It's OK,' he said, quitting the limp, when he was sure he'd got her attention. 'I'm not gonna start on about us getting back together again or nothing. I just wondered

... is it true what they're saying about Simon?'

'Depends who "they" are and what exactly they're saying, doesn't it?'

'About how Simon reckons Luke Harris is trying to kill him?'

'And who told you that?'

'Briony, Amrit...everyone knows!'

'Yeah,' said Kirsty. 'Well, the cops reckon some screws were loose.'

'In Simon's head?' said Jamie. 'Awww, don't storm off. I was joking!'

'Oh sure, it's really funny, Jamie,' said Kirsty, stopping and turning to face him. 'Tampering with someone's bike. Almost killing them.'

'Yeah, but Amrit reckons it's all rubbish. He reckons the screws must have worked loose on Sunday night, when Simon was pratting around doing wheelies and stuff, showing off, bouncing the bike over ramps.'

'They might have done,' said Kirsty. 'And I think Simon's wrong about Luke. But it's sort of co-incidental, isn't it? Simon gets attacked in the park, and then his brakes fail.'

'Loads of people have bike accidents or get mugged. They don't all go around saying it's personal and someone's trying to kill 'em, do they? I mean, drama king or what?'

'Then there's the matter of the texts and phone calls,' said Kirsty, wondering why she was bothering to try to explain to Jamie at all. 'I got one myself, remember.'

A slight blink of his eyes, a faint change of expression, jolted her.

'It *was* you, wasn't it?' she said. 'I was right all along. wasn't I?'

'Yeah,' said Jamie, averting his eyes. 'Look, I'm sorry.'

'Sorry! You make sleazy bloody phone calls, scare me half to death and you say you're sorry!'

'*One* phone call!' said Jamie. 'I was pissed off with you going off with Simon and everything. I didn't mean to scare you or nothing. I was just mucking about. I didn't think—'

'You never do!'

'I was gonna tell you,' said Jamie. 'I mean I felt really bad about it after I'd done it but you were so mad at me already...look I'm really, really sorry. Don't tell no one, will you? My dad'd kill me if he thought I'd done summat like that!'

'And I suppose you sent those texts to Simon, as well?'

'No!' said Jamie. 'That weren't me, honest. I don't even know Simon's number, do I?'

'I don't know,' said Kirsty. 'But this is important, right? I need you to tell me the truth. Did you send those texts?'

'No! He probably made them up, didn't he?'

Kirsty shook her head as she left Jamie and went to her music lesson. She didn't know what to believe, who to believe anymore. If Jamie had made the phone call and sent the texts, if the stabbing was a random

134

mugging, if the screws worked loose on their own, then maybe there was nothing to worry about. But if not, where did that leave them? Was someone really trying to scare Simon, kill him even? It didn't seem possible.

'Kirsty,' said her clarinet teacher, as she hit yet another wrong note. 'We're supposed to be practising our grade five piece, not impersonating a dying wildebeest.'

'Sorry,' said Kirsty.

'OK, try again, from the beginning and concentrate this time.'

Somehow Kirsty managed to concentrate for the remaining ten minutes of her lesson but the moment she got outside and caught sight of Jamie across the playground, it all came back, a tangled mass of impossibilities knotting themselves in her head. Even the certainties seemed improbable. The idea that Jamie had been jealous enough, wound up enough, to make that phone call. How crazy was that?

Kirsty knew about jealousy, the mere thought of Laura Trent was enough to send green steam hissing out of her nostrils, even now, but she wouldn't start making threatening calls for heaven's sake. And surely Jamie wasn't capable of moving beyond the stupid phone call stage? No! Don't even go there. Jamie wasn't the knife-wielding type and he didn't even know about Simon's bike. Briony was around when the bike was being fixed but she wouldn't have the strength to stab anyone, would she? And why would she want to? She was besotted with Simon. If Briony

135

was going to stab anyone, Kirsty knew exactly who the victim would be!

Luke seemed the obvious suspect. He'd been hanging round Oakfields. He could easily have come back and sabotaged the bike. She could see why Simon was convinced but surely even Luke wasn't that psychotic, was he? Sure he'd attacked his stepfather but that was self-defence, in a way, wasn't it? There was no real reason, no motive for trying to kill Simon!

Her own suspicions kept lurching back towards that creepy neighbour, Mac. Or, if not Mac, someone else who'd been freaked by Simon's questions. Someone who'd been watching Simon, following him. She'd almost convinced herself but on Thursday another possibility reared up, an explanation that seemed horribly plausible.

She'd been to see Simon after school. He was back at Oakfields, confined to bed and in a foul mood because the police had interviewed Luke but then let him go. Not only that but Simon had missed the visit to his dad, which had been put back for another two weeks. Kirsty had tried to cheer him up, tried to keep off the topic of his accidents but it had been hopeless and all she'd got in response were sulks and snarls.

'Do you have to watch me like that?' he said, as he picked at the plate of sandwiches Jaz had brought up for him. 'I hate people watching me eat.'

'Fine,' Kirsty had said, as she got up. 'Do you want me to come round tomorrow?'

'No point,' said Simon. 'I've got my hypnotherapy at three.'

'You're still going to that? You don't really look—'

'I said I was, didn't I?' he'd snapped.

It was quiet as Kirsty left Simon's room. She guessed most people were outside but, as she reached the bottom of the stairs and was about to pass the small lounge, she heard voices. Voices she recognised, voices that made her stop and listen.

'But what if Paul and me are right?' Roz was saying. 'This therapy's just gonna make it worse, isn't it?'

'I can't believe,' said Jaz, so quietly that Kirsty had to move closer to the door to hear her properly, 'that Simon tampered with his own bike, let alone stabbed himself in the back and bashed his own face against a wall!'

'He used to do the head bashing stuff all the time when he was younger,' said Roz, casually. 'And the stab wound was on his shoulder, not his back. Paul reckons it could be done. Simon's bloody inventive when he wants to be, believe me. Al agrees with us and even Colin thinks it's possible.'

'Colin?' said Jaz. 'You've already spoken to Simon's social worker about this?'

'I know we're right,' said Roz, ignoring the question. 'I mean we're not saying Simon's trying to top himself or even do serious damage. It's just attention-seeking, isn't it?'

'Pretty drastic attention-seeking,' said Jaz.

'He's done worse,' said Roz. 'Stuff you'd barely

believe. And it makes sense, doesn't it? If he's started the playing dead business again, like I thought, stabbing himself for real isn't exactly a massive jump, is it? Paul said all along that Simon would kick off again big time if he started seeing his dad. I mean it stands to reason. Dredging it all up. Going around asking a load of stupid questions. Hearing stuff about his mum he's better off not knowing. There's no way Simon can cope with that sort of pressure.'

Roz was right, Kirsty thought, leaning against the wall. The idea that Simon could be self-harming and to that extent made her feel ill but it made sense. Total sense. At least to anyone who knew Simon.

'The thing is,' said Roz. 'If he carries on like this, he's gonna do himself some real harm, isn't he? I've seen it all before. If nobody stops him, the attention-seeking builds up and up till—'

'OK,' said Jaz. 'I get the picture. But even if he's done it all himself, I prefer not to see it as attention-seeking.'

'How the hell else can you see it?'

'As a cry for help,' said Jaz. 'And, hopefully, help is what the therapy will provide. That's why I'm keen for him to keep the appointment.'

Kirsty moved back as she heard footsteps moving towards the door but no one came out. Someone, probably Roz, was pacing around.

'He won't even let us go with him,' Roz said. 'I've offered, Paul's offered and all Simon says is it's something he wants to do on his own!'

138

'I've offered too,' said Jaz. 'But he doesn't want anyone. So we have to respect that. Just stand back for a while and let him do it. We're lucky; the clinic's only two streets away. Simon hasn't got a new mobile yet so I'll ask the clinic to phone me when he arrives and when he leaves, just in case there's a problem but there won't be, I'm sure. He's really keen to go. He won't muck around.'

It sounded as though the conversation was coming to a close but then Jaz spoke again.

'Simon tells me Paul's been helping him out. Talking to the solicitor.'

'Yes,' said Roz. 'Why?'

'Nothing,' said Jaz. 'Just wondered if anything had come of it.'

'Not yet,' said Roz. 'And I don't suppose it will, neither. Total waste of bloody time if you ask me. But at least Paul's tried.'

The conversation really was over now so Kirsty hurried past the door, trying not to squeal as a pain shot through her sore foot. How could Jaz be so casual about it all? Whether Simon was in danger from himself or someone else, it was still danger. But presumably Oakfields and the therapist knew what they were doing, didn't they? She'd just have to leave them to it and hope for the best.

Chapter 12

She just couldn't do it. She couldn't leave it alone. Couldn't leave Simon alone. It was getting completely stupid, compulsive almost, Kirsty thought, as she walked towards the clinic after school on Friday. He should be finished about four. It couldn't possibly do any harm to go and meet him, ask how it had gone. Or maybe it would be better not to speak to him. Not to let him see her. Just hang back. Check that he was OK, heading home towards Oakfields and not about to do anything stupid.

The clinic was on a tree-lined street of tall Victorian semis. The clinic side of the street had double yellow lines but on her side there were cars parked along the kerb. With the cars and the trees it should be easy to stay out of sight. She looked up ahead and over to the right to see if she could see Simon coming out. She couldn't but she saw something else, someone else. A white van parked on the yellow lines. Someone was leaning against the back doors of the van. Paul. Simon's uncle had obviously had the same idea as her, to meet Simon, to make sure he was all right. She was about to cross over and speak to Paul when something stopped her.

Not one single thing. Nothing definite. Nothing she

could actually pin down. There was the van, for a start. She'd seen it before, of course, parked outside Oakfields but she'd vaguely thought then, as she was thinking now, that there was something familiar about it. That she'd seen it somewhere before.

Then there was Paul himself. He looked different somehow. He was smoking. She'd never seen him smoke before. But it wasn't just that. He looked tense, nervous. Not his face, she wasn't close enough to see his expression, but the way he was leaning, then standing, then leaning again. Throwing down the cigarette, quickly lighting another, looking round all the time, as if he was expecting someone.

Of course he was expecting someone! He was looking for Simon, wasn't he, like she was? So why was he looking up and down the street? Maybe Roz was joining him. Maybe he was just bored with waiting. It wasn't anything weird or creepy. What the hell was wrong with her? Why did everything about Simon wind her up, make her so paranoid? Paul was tense because he was worried about Simon. Nothing more, nothing less.

He was moving now, towards the clinic gates but after only a few steps he turned and walked back towards the van, as Kirsty slipped behind one of the trees. Get a grip, she told herself as she leant against the trunk. Stop behaving like some sort of demented spy! Just go and talk to the man!

Yet she couldn't. Partly because he was already moving back towards the clinic again and partly because something was holding her there. A thought, a series of thoughts, niggling, gnawing, merging to form tantalising pictures, which wouldn't quite come into focus. And when they did, when she finally realised where it was all leading, she could barely believe what she'd conjured up.

'Are you all right?' the therapist said. 'How do you feel?'

'OK,' said Simon. 'Sort of. It's weird.'

'What is?'

'I wasn't asleep. I can remember what we talked about.'

The therapist smiled.

'I told you,' she said. 'People have a lot of wrong ideas about this sort of therapy. It's really only about creating a sense of deep relaxation, so you can access thoughts and feelings that wouldn't normally be available. You look disappointed!'

'No. Well, yes, sort of. I mean we just talked about ordinary stuff, didn't we? Recent stuff.'

'I wouldn't say your accidents or going to see your dad were exactly ordinary.'

'Yeah, but I know all that without your help, don't I? What I want is the things I don't remember! Things from way back. The sort of stuff I see in my dreams only I want 'em clearer.'

'Don't rush it,' said the therapist. 'This was only the first session. We need to work our way back slowly. I'm sure it'll happen. You seem very receptive but you just have to be patient.'

Patient! He was sick of being patient, waiting for things that didn't happen, but he nodded, as the therapist glanced at her watch, then stood up to show him out.

'I think you were very brave to come at all,' she said, looking at his bandaged arm as she opened the door. 'The state you're in!'

It was funny, Simon thought, as he left the clinic, he hadn't felt any pain or discomfort while he'd been talking to the therapist but now it was starting to come back, the throbbing in his arm, the tightness around his face, the dull pain behind his eyes. It was time for his next lot of painkillers. Kept at Oakfields, of course. They didn't trust him with tablets! He was beginning to wonder whether he could even make it back to Oakfields. He felt tired, drained and every step was a massive effort, so utterly exhausting that he was actually pleased to see Paul lurking at the gate, waiting for him.

'Hi,' said Paul. 'Thought you might want a bit of company after all. We'll pick Roz and the kids up, eh? Go for a pizza or something.'

Simon didn't feel remotely hungry but he was too tired to argue.

'OK,' he said. 'But I need to stop off at Oakfields first. Get my tablets.'

'Sure,' said Paul. 'So how did the hypnosis go then?'

Kirsty stood, clutching her mobile, certain now that she remembered the first time she'd seen Paul's van. It was the day she'd visited Simon at Oakfields, the day she'd been convinced someone was watching her. Her suspicions had focused on the pedestrians behind her, who'd turned out to be Al and Dave. But there was something else. A van had whizzed past, splashing her with mud. A white van with bold green writing. She hadn't noticed what the writing said and there were probably loads of similar vans around, of course. Even if it was Paul's, it didn't prove anything, did it? Except perhaps that she was cracking up. But if you put it together with other stuff . . .

She stepped back, automatically, as she saw Simon and Paul turn out of the clinic and head towards the van. Simon was walking towards the van with Paul! What was she supposed to do? Phone the cops? No that was just too crazy. Why shouldn't Simon go off with his uncle? Unless she was right. But she couldn't be, could she? It was like Roz had said the other day. Too many thrillers. So maybe she should just go over and join them. But it was already too late for that. They were getting in the van.

Phone Oakfields then, in five minutes or so to check that Simon was back. That couldn't do any harm and would, hopefully, put her mind at rest. Better still, she could walk round and, by the time she got there, Paul would have delivered Simon safely, wouldn't he? OK, so the van was setting off in the wrong direction but it would be tricky to turn in a street like this. Paul was probably going to double back.

Kirsty was so busy watching and fretting as the van finally pulled out that she barely noticed another vehicle, a blue car, stopping right beside her.

'I thought we were gonna stop off at Oakfields,' Simon moaned. 'The pain's making me feel sick.'

'Sorry, mate,' said Paul. 'Completely forgot but Roz'll have some painkillers in her bag. Carries 'em around 'cos of her migraines.'

'My mum used to get a lot of headaches,' said Simon. 'Maybe it's a family thing.'

'Is that something you talked about with this therapy woman then?'

'No,' said Simon. 'We didn't go over anything like that but it's funny 'cos since I came out, all sorts of stuff's been coming into my head.'

'Like what?'

'I dunno really, bits of pictures, memories I suppose. They're there, and then they go again, like someone's holding flashcards up. It's weird.'

'Trouble is, you don't know how weird, do you? You don't know what this therapy's gonna do to you. I really think you should give it up, Si.'

'So you've said, fifty million times. Where we going anyway? I thought we were picking Roz up.'

'Meeting up, not picking up,' said Paul. 'There's this pub I know out in one of the villages. Does great food.'

'You said we were having pizza.'

'Pizza's their speciality,' said Paul, as they headed out

145

of town. 'I mean, it's not really me who wants you to give up on this therapy stuff, it's Roz.'

'You always do that.'

'What?'

'Blame each other!'

'I'm not blaming anyone! I'm just saying that Roz has had about as much as she can take. I love Roz, yer know. I don't want nothing upsetting her and the kids. And if you start kicking off again because of this rubbish—'

'It's not rubbish and I won't kick off.'

'Won't you? Roz thinks you already have. And Oakfields agree with her. I mean, if it turns out that you've been harming yourself.'

'Harming myself? What you on about?'

Paul glanced at him, nodding towards his arm.

'If those injuries are self-inflicted.'

'They're not! You think I'd do all this to myself? Are you mad or what?'

'It's not *my* sanity that's in question, is it, Si?' said Paul. 'If you carry on like this you're gonna end up in a psychiatric unit, you know that, don't you?'

'So? If I do, it's tough, innit? I'm not self-harming and I'm not giving up the therapy. If there's a chance, any chance at all that I'll remember summat, then it's worth it.'

'Mmm,' said Paul. 'I had a feeling you might say that. Blimey, Si, you look really pale, you're not gonna throw up, are you?'

'It's you, goin' on at me all the time! And the pain. Feels like I've got a dozen rats gnawing through my arm.'

146

'Hang on,' said Paul. 'Have a look in that compartment there. I've got a feeling Roz might have left some of her tablets. Wrapped in a bit of tinfoil. And I think there's a drink too.'

'You're sure these are OK?' said Simon, opening the foil. 'How long have they been lying around?'

'I don't know but they're only Paracetamol or something. Won't be as strong as the stuff you're taking but they'll do for now.'

'The Coke's a bit flat,' said Simon, taking a sip before swallowing one of the tablets. 'Want some?'

'No, you drink it. Don't want you choking on the pills.'

Jaz turned left, off the country road and onto an even narrower one with plenty of twists and turns which made it easy to stay out of view.

'I don't believe this,' she told Kirsty. 'I don't believe I'm doing this.'

'It's a bit odd though, isn't it?' said Kirsty. 'Them driving out to the middle of nowhere like this.'

'Odd, yeah,' said Jaz. 'But not what you'd call criminal. Why don't we just phone Paul? I'm sure I've got his number,' she added, indicating the mobile holder.

'In a bit,' said Kirsty. 'Let's just see what happens.'

'Nothing's going to happen!'

'So why did you agree to follow them?'

Jaz laughed.

'I always wanted to be a spy, I guess. Or was it that you didn't exactly give me much choice? I pulled up to

147

say "hi" and the next minute you're in the car telling me to follow that van! It's like a cross between James Bond and a Carry On film!'

'I know,' said Kirsty. 'And I'm going to feel such a prat when it turns out to be nothing but you can see what I'm getting at, can't you?'

'Sort of,' said Jaz.

'It's not just the way Paul was behaving outside the clinic,' Kirsty insisted. 'He was definitely around the bike, wasn't he? And if you think about it, there was only him or Simon who could have mucked with it.'

'Mmm,' said Jaz. 'I'm not sure about that. Anybody at Oakfields could have done it. But go on.'

'Right, well, Paul was allegedly finishing a job when Simon was stabbed but I don't think the police checked. He could easily have sent the texts and could definitely have been watching Simon.'

'So could any number of people,'said Jaz. 'Like me for a start! But what you don't have is any sort of motive. Why should Paul want to harm his own nephew?'

'I don't know,' said Kirsty. 'It's just that Paul seems pretty uptight about what Simon's doing. Always tried to stop him seeing his dad. Maybe Paul and Roz are covering something up.'

'I know they are,' said Jaz, thoughtfully. 'Quite a lot, probably. Things they haven't even told us. But they think they're doing it in Simon's best interests. They're trying to protect him.'

'So you think I'm crazy, right?' said Kirsty.

'No,' said Jaz. 'But I'm hoping you've just got an over-active imagination. I'm hoping that Paul's just doing what you and me were doing. Looking out for Simon, making sure he didn't do anything stupid but—'

'But what?'

'Well, there *is* a sort of reason I'm going along with all this. Something happened the other day. I didn't think too much of it at the time but after what you've just said, I suppose it might mean something.'

'Well,' said Kirsty. 'Are you going to tell me what it was?'

'Hang on,' said Jaz, as they drove round a corner at the top of a hill and looked down onto the road snaking out in front, 'I think we've lost them!'

Chapter 13

'What now?' said Simon. 'Why have we stopped?'

The pain had eased but he felt so tired, he was struggling to stay awake.

'Must have taken a wrong turning,' said Paul. 'I was sure it was this one.'

'This isn't going anywhere. It's a dead end,' said Simon, looking at the gateway ahead, leading to a path through a wood.

'Exactly,' said Paul, doing a three-point turn.

But instead of driving on, he stopped again, turned off the engine and looked at Simon.

'What!' Simon yelled. 'What yer looking at me for?'

'We need to talk.'

'You haven't stopped talking since we left the bloody clinic. And you're wasting your time.'

'Yeah, I know,' said Paul. 'That's what we need to talk about.'

'Give up, will yer and just drive. You're doing my bloody head in now. Oh God!'

'What?'

'I dunno. I feel totally knackered. My head's spinning and I feel sick again.'

'Have another drink.'

Simon swigged the warm, flat Coke, almost draining the bottle.

'Uggh,' he said. 'Look, can we just go now? Forget the meal. Just take me back before I puke up.'

'Yeah, all right, mate. Calm down.'

'Yer still lookin' at me! What is it? What's going on?'

There was something strange about Paul. His face was going in and out of focus but it wasn't just that. There was something about his expression like it was angry, sad, happy... all mixed-up, changing, confused. Like he was up to something. Something bad.

Watching Paul, trying to work it out, was making Simon feel weak, faint. The tiredness, the dizziness, coming in waves every few seconds. Worse than when he'd come off his bike. Like being drunk, drugged up, hung over, all at once. The tablets should be helping by now but they weren't.

'Them tablets?' said Simon. 'You sure they were OK?'

'Yeah,' said Paul.

'Well something's got to me.'

'You sure you haven't taken something, yourself?'

'Uh?'

'Well the state you've been in recently,' said Paul. 'You could have done, couldn't you? Tried to overdose? Another way of attention-seeking.'

'I haven't,' said Simon. 'I told you. I haven't done nothing to myself.'

What was Paul on about? Why wouldn't he just let it drop? Take him home? But he didn't. He just sat there, shaking his head slightly, his eyes hard, steely but misty at the same time, as though he was about to cry.

'But people think you have,' Paul was saying, as if talking to himself. 'I've made sure of that. So they wouldn't be surprised if you tried to OD, would they? And...if I couldn't get you to hospital in time.'

Paul's cloudy eyes rested, momentarily, on the almost empty Coke bottle.

'The drink?' said Simon, struggling to focus, struggling to think.

Overdose. Tablets. Drink. Paul. Paul had given them to him.

'There was summat in the drink? Them tablets weren't just painkillers?'

Simon laughed as he said it. He didn't mean to. It just happened. It was silly. Like a film or something. Funny. Crazy. Unreal.

'I'll get rid of the bottle,' Paul said. 'Say you started acting strange, then passed out on me. Yeah...'

Simon blinked as the words sliced through the fog, the dizziness. It wasn't funny or crazy anymore. A sudden surge of energy shot through him as if his body was acting all on its own, pushing open the van door, half scrambling, half falling out, before he had time to think what he was doing or why he was doing it.

He dropped onto his knees, pushing his fingers into his mouth, deep into the back of his throat, making himself vomit, knowing it was too late. He couldn't stand, couldn't get up again, couldn't even stay on his

152

knees. As he slumped forward onto the damp ground, he was vaguely aware of Paul crouching beside him. Simon managed to roll onto his side, resting on his good arm, trying to breathe, trying to stay awake.

'What've you given me?' he managed to say. 'Why?'

His own voice sounded faint, distant, drawn out, like it was barely there at all but Paul's sounded loud, far too loud.

'Bit of a cocktail, I'm afraid, Si. Stuff I managed to get hold of. I had to do it. You wouldn't listen. You wouldn't see reason. I tried. I tried everything. Tried to talk to you. Tried to frighten you. But you wouldn't give up.'

What was Paul on about? What was he saying? Frighten? Didn't make sense. Focus. Focus. Think. Not happening. Couldn't be happening. Frighten?

'The bike?' Simon said. 'The other stuff?'

'Warnings. But you wouldn't take no notice. Going on about your bloody dreams. Digging around. Stirring up trouble.'

'I don't get it.'

'It doesn't matter now,' said Paul, rubbing at his hands so hard that Simon could hear the rough skin scratching against Paul's rings.

Simon forced his eyes open wide, tried to look at Paul but it didn't help; the face was just a blur, a hazy whiteness like it wasn't really a face at all. Dream. It was like the dream face, melting, distorting...

'Don't shout, Mum, don't do that, I didn't see anything, I didn't see, I'm sorry, leave me alone!'

153

Did I see? Did I know? Did I always know? Memories not dreams. Blotting them out. Things I didn't want to see. Didn't want to remember. Paul and Mum. Mum and Paul.

'NO! It wasn't you. YouwithMum. I saw someone. Couldn't be. Sayitwasn't...'

Words, disjointed, dripping from his mouth, floating away.

'It was a mistake, Simon. It was all a stupid, bloody mistake.'

Everything floating away. Don't sleep. Don't lose it. Got to listen. Got to try. Got to ask him. Mistake. Not real. Mouth won't work. Hands, touching my head, stroking my hair. Can't move away. Can't get him off me.

'Simon?'

Quiet now. Hands moving away. Rustling. Doing something. What? Try to see. Jacket. Taking jacket off. Why? Folding it. Looking at me again. Close. Too close. Not happening. Dream. Dreams feel real.

'I'm sorry. I'm sorry, Si. I had to do it. I had to stop you. I couldn't let you wreck everything for Roz and me. Not after all this time. Not after ten years. She was gonna do that. Your mum. She was going to tell Roz. And your dad! She was gonna tell everyone, wreck everything. I couldn't let her do it. I loved Roz. Your mum was just a cheap little...'

Don't listen. Don't listen to him. Don't let him say that.

'She offered it, Simon. After your dad left. She wouldn't leave me alone. I wanted to stop. You were

154

gettin' older. You were gonna notice something. I told her we had to stop but she just started screaming at me. Threatening to tell. The knife was there on the side. I . . . '

Don't tell me. Won't listen. Not true. Not real.

' . . . a bit of luck, your dad turning up. It was so easy. So easy, Si, once the cops got hold of him. I tried to make it up to you. Why couldn't you see? You were better off without them. Why couldn't you leave it alone? They were scum, both of them. Just scum.'

Stop him. Got to stop him.

Simon tried to reach out but his arm only twitched uselessly, lifelessly. He could feel Paul's breath on his face. Then something else. Something heavier. Soft. Pressing. Jacket. Pressing into his face. Pain in his eyes, his ears, his throat, his brain, bulging, bursting . . .

'They could have gone down there,' Kirsty said, pointing to the track on the right as they retraced their route.

'Doesn't look hopeful,' said Jaz. 'But I'll turn round, give it a shot. Then if we don't catch up with them we're going to stop playing cops and robbers, give Paul a ring. Find out where the hell they are. What's going on.'

'Yeah, all right,' said Kirsty. 'But what were you going to tell me? About what happened the other day?'

'It's probably nothing,' said Jaz, as she swung the car round in a lay-by. 'But you know Paul was going to talk to the police and the solicitor for Simon?'

'Yeah.'

'Well the solicitor phoned about something else and I

asked him whether he thought any of the stuff Simon had dredged up was relevant. I thought it might cheer Simon up if there'd been any sort of breakthrough but—'

'But the solicitor didn't know what you were talking about, right?'

'Right,' said Jaz. 'At first I thought Paul hadn't got round to it or only said he'd go to shut Simon up but when I checked with Roz, she seemed pretty confident Paul had been and I thought it was sort of odd that Paul had lied to Roz.'

Kirsty nodded, as Jaz turned onto the track. She'd overheard that conversation. But, even if Paul had lied about the solicitor, the other part of the conversation, what Roz had said about Simon self-harming, still made sense. Probably a whole lot more sense than her own crazy theory.

'Bloody hell!' said Jaz, suddenly slamming on the brakes so hard that Kirsty shot forward, saved only by the restraint of her seat belt. 'What's he doing?'

The van was what Kirsty saw first. Not far from them. Then the figures. Paul scrambling up, looking at them, rocking slightly, clutching a jacket or something to his chest, like a comfort blanket. Simon lying on the ground. Still. Far too still. Kirsty clicked off her seat belt, reached for the door handle.

'Don't!' said Jaz. 'Don't go out there. Lock the door.'

'But—'

Jaz didn't wait. She'd already locked the doors from her side, picked up the phone.

'What about Simon?' Kirsty screamed, as Jaz made the emergency call. 'We can't just leave him!'

Jaz was talking quickly but calmly. Explaining where they were, what was happening. How could she be so cool with Simon lying there, with Paul standing over him, looking towards the woods, the van, planning his escape?

'Right,' said Jaz, throwing the phone to Kirsty. 'I'm getting out. You stay here.'

Kirsty had no intention of staying but as Jaz unlocked the doors, Paul suddenly made his move.

'Oh my God . . . Jaz!' Kirsty yelled.

Paul was getting into the van. Starting the engine. What did he think he was doing? He couldn't get past them. They were blocking the lane. It was far too narrow.

Jaz looked up, closed the door, and then quickly slammed the car into reverse, moving back at the same time as the van shot forward. Jaz was reversing fast, veering wildly, scraping the hedge. But it wasn't fast enough. They were nearly back at the junction but they wouldn't make it in time. The van was almost upon them.

Kirsty barely had time to register the wall of white when she felt the impact. Instinctively her hands shot up, covering her face. A thud, then another and another. Paul was pulling back, driving forward, ramming them again and again. Noise. Too much noise. Horns, brakes, her screams, Jaz's screams, filling the car and all the time, behind Kirsty's closed eyes, the image of Simon. An image that shattered as their car suddenly picked up speed, swerved, skidded, jolted, stopped.

Stopped.

Kirsty's hands dropped from her face to see branches, light branches, leaves, masses of leaves, strewn across the windscreen. Hedge. They were stuck in a hedge. Far side of the junction. Facing the track. The van out in the middle of the road, spinning round to the right. Something else. Tractor. Coming at Paul. Van, tractor, meshing together, van crumpling. Man jumping down from the tractor. Dog barking. Collie. Black and white, following the man. Jaz running towards the van before Kirsty even knew she'd left the car.

Kirsty snatched at the handle, pushed the door. It was open but not far, caught in the tangle of hedge. Kirsty pushed further, scrambled out, hearing sirens now, in the distance, getting closer. How would they get through, with the van, the tractor, blocking the road? How would they get to Simon? Rushing past the vehicles, the farmer and Jaz, Kirsty ran across the road, down the track, back towards Simon. Ignoring the pain in her foot, running faster than she'd ever done, her heart pounding in her chest, echoing in her head, as sobs rose, stuck in her throat, threatening to choke her.

Simon hadn't moved. He was still lying there, semi-curled, like that day in the park. No blood this time. No sign of breathing. She lay down, her head on his chest, her hand reaching for his wrist. There was a pulse, she was sure. Very faint but it was there. But no breathing. She couldn't feel him breathing at all.

Chapter 14

Kirsty heard footsteps running lightly towards her but didn't look up until someone gripped her shoulders, pulling her away. She watched, helplessly, as Jaz dropped down beside Simon, rolling him onto his back, pinching his nose, putting her face over his, breathing into his mouth. Stopping, starting, putting the heel of her hand onto Simon's chest, pressing, breathing into his mouth again. Breathing, pressing, breathing, for what seemed like hours but could only have been seconds until the paramedics arrived, on foot, carrying a stretcher, equipment.

Jaz stood up, clutched hold of Kirsty, both of them crying, as the paramedics took over. Kirsty wanted to push forward, see what was happening but Jaz held her back.

'Let them get on with it,' she said, her voice, faint and choked. 'It's the best way to help him. There's nothing you can do.'

The police officers, who arrived as Simon was being carried away, told her the same thing, leading her back to the road, ushering her into the back of a police car. There were a million things Kirsty wanted to ask, needed to know about Simon, about Paul but no words would come. All she could do was cry.

'You're in shock,' she heard someone say. 'We're going to get you to hospital, OK?'

Kirsty couldn't even nod, couldn't make her head move. Her whole body was trembling, freezing cold. A police lady covered her with a blanket but it didn't help.

'Mum,' Kirsty finally managed to murmur. 'I want my mum.'

Jaz sat on the edge of Simon's hospital bed.

'You're looking better,' she said. 'A lot better.'

'Don't feel it,' said Simon. 'How long have I been here, this time? I've lost track.'

'Eight days.'

Simon let his head flop back on the pillow and closed his eyes so Jaz wouldn't see the tears. The tears that kept coming. All the time. He didn't have to think about anything. It was as though he couldn't think. As though his mind had completely shut down and all that was left was the hole, the black hole he couldn't break free of.

'It's all right,' said Jaz, touching his hand as tears trickled out from beneath his closed lids.

He found himself gripping Jaz's hand, like he'd done with Kirsty's . . . when was it? This morning? Yesterday? Jaz and Kirsty were the only people he'd seen. The only ones he wanted to see. There were the doctors and nurses, of course, and the police. He didn't have any choice about seeing them.

Roz. He wanted to see Roz. But she wouldn't come. They'd told him Roz was ill. Too ill, too shocked to leave the house. But he knew it wasn't that. She was blaming him. For what had happened to Paul. Paul. The name hit him like a physical blow to his ribs, pain tightening in his chest forcing bile into his throat, making him retch.

'Hey,' said Jaz, passing him the grey cardboard bowl. 'Come on. Try to breathe. Deep breaths.'

'I can't get my head round it,' Simon said. 'What he did. To me. To my mum. To my dad. Ten years. Ten years he carried on like nothing was wrong.'

'Maybe not quite,' said Jaz, quietly. 'I think it was always with him. Eating away, corrupting, like these things do. Blurring the line between sanity and madness, until he thought it was logical, reasonable to try... to do what he almost did to you.'

'You mean he's gonna get off by saying he's nuts?'

'No,' said Jaz. 'He won't get off but he'll probably claim diminished responsibility.'

'But he planned it!' said Simon, the words, the images exploding in his head all at once. 'The screws on the bike, the drugs in the drink. Making out like I was doing it all to myself! Getting people on his side. How can that be diminished anything? He knew what he was doing. And my mum. He knew what he was doing to her, too.'

Simon leant over the bowl as the dizziness, the sickness came again.

'Is it always gonna be like this?' he asked Jaz, as she helped him sit back again. 'Throwing up every time I hear his name. Every time I think about it.'

'No,' said Jaz. 'It won't always be that way, I promise.'

'I'll have to give evidence,' he said. 'At the trial. How can I do that? I won't be able to face it. I know I won't. What about Ben and Ellie? They're gonna go through everything I went through, aren't they? Worse I suppose. Ellie's like so close to him...'

He banged his head against the pillow, then let his head slump into his hands, covering his face, blotting it all out. But it wouldn't go.

'And Roz?' he said, looking up at Jaz again. 'How's she gonna cope? What are they going to do? Will they move away? I mean how much does she know? Does she even believe it? About him and Mum? Did she ever think... ever suspect? How could he do that with Mum? How could he?'

Jaz was shaking her head, slowly, as if she didn't know which question to answer first. But it didn't matter because she couldn't. She couldn't answer any of them. No one could. Because there weren't any answers. Only questions. Hundreds of them. The minute he started thinking, talking, out they came, tumbling over each other.

'What's going to happen to me? I can't stay here, can I? And my dad? The cops won't tell me nothing.'

A slight blink of Jaz's eyes caught his attention.

'What?' he said. 'What is it? You know something, don't you?'

'It's what I came to tell you,' said Jaz. 'The police thought it might be better if I told you. I wasn't sure you were ready but—'

'What?' Simon yelled again. 'Tell me.'

'They're releasing him,' said Jaz.

'When?'

'Tomorrow.'

Kirsty stood staring out of the lounge window, waiting for the car. She wasn't ready for any of this; it was all happening too fast. In the month that Simon had been in hospital, all the decisions had been made. And now it was over. Jaz was collecting Simon from hospital and bringing him here to say goodbye, before picking up his dad from the hostel, where he'd been staying, and driving them both to Yorkshire.

Yorkshire. It wasn't that far. Britain was a small enough country, for heaven's sake.

'We'll keep in touch, yeah?' she'd said to Simon, when she'd first heard the plans.

He'd nodded, even smiled, which was rare from Simon these days, but he hadn't meant it. And she'd understood. In a way. He was making a new start. A completely new start. He didn't want anything getting in the way.

Social services had fixed up a foster home for Simon and a flat for his dad. The idea was that they'd see each

163

other, regularly, building up slowly to see how things worked out. Simon was going to quit school, get an apprenticeship of some sort and his dad had already had a job fixed up. Part-time at first, until he got settled.

'I think we'll be OK in the end, me and Dad,' Simon had said, in a moment of optimism. 'We should be. Do you know how many flaming counsellors and social workers we're gonna have between us?'

Kirsty had shaken her head and laughed when he told her.

'I'm sorry,' she'd said, immediately. 'I know it's not really funny. I mean it's good that you're going to get all that support.'

'Yeah, well, I don't like people meddling but we'll probably need it. Dad's like totally confused. As though he can't believe he's out. I'm not even sure he likes it much. Jaz reckons he's a bit...what do you call it? When you're scared of open spaces?'

'Agoraphobic?'

'Yeah, that's right. He had a panic attack in the street the other day. On the way to see me. Ended up walking into the police station, trying to hand himself in, the pillock! But you see what I mean, don't you? How's he gonna manage to work like that? It's not gonna be easy, is it? But we're like, getting on really well, so that's a start, isn't it?'

It *was* a start but would it be enough? Kirsty's hands gripped the windowsill as Jaz's car pulled up.

Amazingly it hadn't suffered that much damage and the garage had mended it within a week. Machines were obviously a whole lot easier to fix than people.

Simon was getting out of the car. He'd lost weight. Quite a lot. He'd been slim to start with but now he was skinny, his face so angular it looked as if it might have been chiselled. The swelling, the bruising from the bike accident had gone and what was left was pallor.

He didn't really look well enough to be out of hospital but the doctors had said he'd been fit enough, physically, for a couple of weeks now. What had kept Simon there had been the depression, the night terrors. The hospital wanted to get his psyche under control before they released him and now they reckoned they had. Kirsty wasn't sure. Even two days ago, when she'd seen him, he'd been really uptight, shouting at her, telling her she didn't understand.

He was right, in a way, she didn't. She'd been over it so many times, in her own head, with Simon, with her parents, with the police, with Jaz and it still barely made any sense.

'Paul seemed so ordinary,' she'd said to Jaz. 'Just a regular bloke.'

'Most killers are,' Jaz had said. 'And most murders are domestic. Statistically, you're in more danger from people you know, people you love, than you ever are from strangers.'

'I'm not talking about statistics!'

'Neither am I, really,' said Jaz. 'I'm talking about the

165

kids I work with. They've all been hurt by people close to them.'

'Not always deliberately! Not like Paul did to Simon.'

'Paul felt trapped,' Jaz had said. 'By what had happened before. I think he'd have done anything to cover up. Anything.'

'But he didn't have to hurt Simon,' Kirsty had said. 'Simon hadn't sussed anything definite. There was only a faint chance that the therapy would help him remember.'

'*Any* chance was too much of a risk for Paul. And the more Simon went on about it all, the more paranoid Paul became.'

The slam of a car door jolted Kirsty into action. She waved at Jaz and Simon before heading for the front door to let them in. But she was too late, Mum was already there, fussing, ushering them in, offering coffee. Jaz followed Mum into the kitchen but Simon veered off into the lounge and Kirsty followed.

'Close the door,' he said.

'Why?'

'I just wanna talk to you. On your own. Without no one listening in.'

'Sounds serious.'

'No,' said Simon, perching on the arm of one of the chairs. 'It isn't. I just wanted to say thanks, I guess.'

'Why? It wasn't me that gave you the kiss of life you know. It was Jaz!'

'Yeah,' said Simon. 'The only time Jaz is ever going to kiss me and I missed it!'

'Oh!' said Kirsty. 'Didn't know you fancied Jaz.'

'Not really,' said Simon. 'It's just a sort of fantasy thing, innit? So don't go telling her or nothing. Anyway don't change the subject. I was trying to talk about you. To say thanks and sorry and stuff.'

'Don't be daft,' said Kirsty.

'I'm not being daft,' said Simon, getting up, moving towards her, pulling something out of his pocket. 'I got you this.'

Kirsty stared at the small bag he'd thrust into her hand.

'Well, Jaz got them for me. But she said you'd like 'em,' Simon mumbled, looking towards the floor.

Kirsty open the bag, took out the earrings. Green. Long, dangly but delicate.

'You didn't have to,' Kirsty found herself saying. 'I mean, I haven't got you anything. I didn't think...'

'Yeah, well,' said Simon, looking up at her. 'I know it sounds weird but I just wanted you to remember summat nice about me instead of all the shit.'

'We don't have to lose touch,' she tried.

'We do,' said Simon, looking round the lounge. ''Cos I'll still be dealing with all the shit, months, years from now and you don't have to. Except for Paul's trial I suppose. They'll want you to give evidence, won't they?'

'I'm not sure,' said Kirsty. 'My written statement might be enough. It depends. I don't suppose you've seen Roz at all?'

Simon shook his head.

'She's still not well enough to see anyone much. Paul's mum and dad are sorting things out. Looking after Ben and Ellie. But they're in a state too. Paul's parents. It's all such a mess. Such a bloody mess.'

Simon's body tensed, as he spoke, then started to sway. He stretched out, clutched the arm of the sofa and sat down.

'Hey,' Kirsty said, hastily taking out her studs and putting the green earrings in, desperate to distract him. 'What do you reckon?'

'Nice,' he said, vacantly.

He was looking at her but not really seeing. He was somewhere else. With his dad? With Paul? With Roz? This was what he was dealing with. Would always be dealing with.

'He'll get through it,' Jaz had told her a couple of days ago. 'It's amazing what people learn to cope with. Horrendous stuff, you'd barely believe. And Simon's stronger than he thinks.'

Kirsty sat down next to him and hugged him. She hadn't known him long, barely a couple of months, but she'd miss him. She felt the pain tightening in her throat, tried to multiply it, tried to imagine the pain, the pain of loss that Simon must feel, all the time, but she couldn't. It was impossible. She felt him gently push her away as the door opened and Jaz came in.

'Ready?' Jaz asked. 'We're a bit late. Your dad's just phoned wondering where we are.'

Simon was already up, walking into the hall, anxious to be gone. He left the house, got into the car, without once looking back.

Maybe one day, Kirsty thought, if things work with his dad, if he gets himself sorted out, maybe he'll get in touch. And he *would* get sorted.

Like Jaz said, Simon was tough. A survivor. He'd be all right. He had to be.